D0150266

Blaze

Dear Reader,

I'm overjoyed to return to my Western roots after visits to other historical venues and romantic suspense. And when I was offered a chance to write for Harlequin Blaze, well, how could I resist?

My hero and heroine, Jared and Samantha, have long haunted me. In truth, they have been demanding my attention for nearly eight years. I've ignored them until now, promising them their day. And this is it.

Sam and Jared are one of the strongest pairs I've ever brought to life. She's the adopted daughter of an outlaw she dearly loves, and Jared is a marshal with a personal vendetta against that same outlaw.

Samantha will do anything, including shooting Jared, to save the man who protected her for most of her life. Jared will do anything to hang the man he believes responsible for the murder of someone dear to him, even if it means breaking the heart of a woman he's coming to love.

Don't miss the fireworks!

Patricia Potter

Patricia Potter

THE LAWMAN

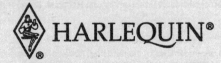

TORONTO • NEW YORK • LONDON
AMSTERDAM • PARIS • SYDNEY • HAMBURG
STOCKHOLM • ATHENS • TOKYO • MILAN • MADRID
PRAGUE • WARSAW • BUDAPEST • AUCKLAND

Recycling programs
for this product may
not exist in your area.

ISBN-13: 978-0-373-79569-7

THE LAWMAN

Copyright © 2010 by Patricia Potter.

All rights reserved. Except for use in any review, the reproduction or utilization of this work in whole or in part in any form by any electronic, mechanical or other means, now known or hereafter invented, including xerography, photocopying and recording, or in any information storage or retrieval system, is forbidden without the written permission of the publisher, Harlequin Enterprises Limited, 225 Duncan Mill Road, Don Mills, Ontario M3B 3K9, Canada.

This is a work of fiction. Names, characters, places and incidents are either the product of the author's imagination or are used fictitiously, and any resemblance to actual persons, living or dead, business establishments, events or locales is entirely coincidental.

This edition published by arrangement with Harlequin Books S.A.

For questions and comments about the quality of this book please contact us at Customer_eCare@Harlequin.ca.

® and TM are trademarks of the publisher. Trademarks indicated with ® are registered in the United States Patent and Trademark Office, the Canadian Trade Marks Office and in other countries.

www.eHarlequin.com

Printed in U.S.A.

ABOUT THE AUTHOR

Patricia Potter is a bestselling and award-winning author of more than sixty books. Her Western romances have received numerous awards, including an *RT Book Reviews* Storyteller of the Year, Career Achievement Award for Western Historical Romance and Best Hero of the Year. She is a seven-time RITA® Award finalist for RWA and a three-time Maggie winner. She is a past president of the Romance Writers of America.

Books by Patricia Potter

Don't miss any of our special offers. Write to us at the following address for information on our newest releases.

Harlequin Reader Service
U.S.: 3010 Walden Ave., P.O. Box 1325, Buffalo, NY 14269
Canadian: P.O. Box 609, Fort Erie, Ont. L2A 5X3

For Carolyn, Barbara and Phyllis for their patience, support and really good advice. I love you guys.

Prologue

Colorado Territory
January, 1866

GUILT WEIGHED like an anvil on his heart.

He should have insisted that Emma wait until he could accompany her from Kansas to Denver. He should have been with her.

Now she was dead, and he was responsible.

Just like before.

"You know her, Marshal?"

Jared Evans heard the question but didn't answer. Instead he picked up the body of the young woman from the inside of the coach and carried her into the office he sometimes shared with Denver's sheriff. He wanted her away from the prying eyes of curious onlookers.

He gently laid her down on the bench and knelt beside her, choking off the growl that started deep in his chest.

Emma. Pretty, smart Emma lay still, her dress stained with blood from a gunshot to the heart. She'd been all he had left of his wife, Sarah, who'd also died from an outlaw's bullet three years earlier. Sisters.

She looked so much like Sarah. The same soft, pretty features and golden hair and blue eyes.

Jared hadn't seen her since he'd returned after the war, only to find his wife, young daughter and brother dead, killed months earlier by Quantrill's bloody murderers. Emma had taken him to the graves. Watched as he'd knelt down and howled in grief.

Emma was engaged then, and he'd left to track down the men who'd killed his family....

He closed his eyes. Sarah's face replaced Emma's in his mind's eye.

"Marshal?"

He turned around.

"You know her, Marshal?" The driver, who'd followed them inside, asked again.

He nodded.

"Wasn't no need to kill her," the driver said. "Wasn't no need for anyone to git killed. I stopped. But one of them bushwhackers tried to kiss her after he took her purse, and she bit him. He just plain shot her, then turned the gun on me. I dropped when it hit my shoulder. Heard someone use the name Thornton."

Thornton. He knew the name. Knew it too damned well. He'd been chasing the Thornton gang for more than eight months. Confederates who didn't know the damn war was over. Been robbing mostly military payrolls all over the territory. The jobs had been meticulously planned.

No one had been killed until now.

He touched Emma's hair and closed her eyes. Rage and a terrible grief warred in his heart. For the second time in his life, he was too late to save someone close to his heart. "I'll get them for you," he said to her. "If it's the last thing I ever do, every one of them will hang."

1

Colorado, 1876

SHOOT HIM!

Samantha Blair's fingers flexed as she watched the tall, lean man approach with an easy, graceful stride. *The man she intended to stop at any cost.*

She had stepped off the crumbling porch of the saloon just seconds earlier and stood in the middle of the rutted street in a stance that was all challenge.

Her long duster coat was confining and hot on this unusually warm day, but it disguised her sex. So did her loose shirt and worn pants. A hat covered her short hair, and she'd pulled the brim down over her forehead to cut the glare from the afternoon sun.

Sweat dampened her leather gloves as she stared across the forty feet that separated her from the man with a hard face and a star on his vest. His skin was deeply browned by the sun, his hair black and his eyes deep set. He looked like a hawk to her, dark and predatory. His grim expression did nothing to allay the impression of deadly competence. He moved with a grace that persisted even as he halted.

She pushed her coat back on the right side. He stopped, stiffened when he saw the gun. The intent.

The dry wind kicked up dust, and a hot sun bore down on her and the man who had hunted Mac, one of the three people in the world she loved, for years. She was a healer, not a killer. But now Mac was helpless. Critically wounded. Defenseless.

Except for her.

Mac didn't know she was here. The sign over the saloon— one of only a few structures left in the small mining town of Gideon's Hope after a disastrous fire—hung drunkenly by a chain, while the rest of the building looked as if it were about to fall in.

In the distance she heard Dawg yowl, as if he knew something was terribly wrong. The old hound would be clawing at the door, desperate to come to her aid.

"Go home," the lanky man said in a soft drawl. "I don't shoot kids."

She stiffened. "I'm not a kid," she retorted. She'd hoped her height would offset the impression of youth. "I've killed before," she added, willing him not to see the lie in her eyes. She hadn't killed, but she was good with targets. Very good. And fast.

She could do this, she reassured herself. She had to do it. She wouldn't let doubt rock her. She didn't want to kill the man. Blue blazes, she didn't want to kill anyone. Just stop him. A bullet in the leg would do. Or arm.

Always go for the heart or head. Hit anything else and your opponent will kill you.

How many times had Mac told her that when he'd taught her to shoot? To protect herself. *Don't ever expect a gunman to give you an advantage. He won't.* And the marshal *was* a gunman. She knew his reputation. Had dreaded it for years.

The lawman took a step toward her. "I don't want trouble. I'm looking for an outlaw."

"There's no outlaw here," she said.

His mouth curved into a half smile. "Then I'll look and be on my way."

"We don't like strangers, and we especially don't like the law," she said.

"Who is we?" he asked, his voice controlled. No fear. But

then he was a lawman, and there was something very sure, very competent in every small movement.

"Don't matter," she replied, trying to keep her voice husky. Her heart pounded. Only the conviction that she alone stood between this man and Mac kept her from turning away.

"It matters to me," he said, taking another step.

It was now or never. If he got past her, then he would go after Mac. Her hand moved to her side, just inches from her Colt.

She had no choice. Mac was like a father to her. Now shattered by three bullet wounds, he lay unconscious in a room inside the saloon. She *had* to protect him. There was no one else. *No one.*

"Look, I have no quarrel with you," he tried again. "I don't even know who the hell you are."

"We don't like strangers," Sam repeated. She tried to hide her abhorrence at what she was doing. The fear that turned her blood cold in the hot temperature.

It's for Mac.

Archie was with Mac now. Archie, another of her "godfathers," was the oldest of the three men who had loved her mother and taken over Sam's care when her mother died. Now he needed glasses to see across the room. He would have tried to help if he knew what was happening. And he would have been killed.

Only she stood between the marshal and Mac.

She'd be damned—or dead—before she'd let this man take Mac to hang.

She could have ambushed him, but that went against everything Mac had told her. Only cowards ambushed.

"Leave," she tried again, hoping her desperation didn't reveal itself in her voice. "There's other guns aimed at you." Even as she voiced the words, she knew he wouldn't retreat. Knew his reputation as a ruthless hunter. Still, she had to try. Her heart pounded so hard she feared he could hear it even from a distance.

"Can't do that," the intruder replied. His lips were twisted into a frown. She tried not to look at his holster. Mac said never look at the holster. Or the hand. Look at the eyes. They told you when your opponent was going to draw.

The eyes. Not the face. Concentrate on the eyes. Dark with a glint of blue. Unblinking.

"I'm a U.S. Marshal looking for Cal Thornton. He might be going by the name of MacDonald these days," the lawman continued. "I don't have a quarrel with anyone else." His voice suddenly hardened as he added, "Unless they interfere."

"Don't know no Thornton," she said. "Or MacDonald, either. And that badge don't mean nothing to me."

His gaze didn't leave her face. "That old man in the livery said the owner of the horse there was in the saloon. Thornton rode that horse. There aren't many pintos like it."

"He's crazy. I won that horse in a wager."

"Then I'll just take a look and move on."

"No," she said flatly.

Something about her answer made his lips twist into a smile.

"Where is he, kid?"

She realized with a sick feeling that she'd confirmed the fact that Mac was here. It didn't make any difference, though. She'd seen him talk to old Burley, then start in the direction of the saloon without hesitation. If he'd ridden this far to find Mac, he wouldn't be stopped by a denial. Only a bullet could do that.

She held her ground as he took another step. His gaze met hers, weighing her. Watching her every move.

"No closer," she said. "I'll shoot."

"Are you sure, kid?" His voice was steady. "I bet you never shot a man before."

Her eyes didn't leave the marshal's face. It looked carved from a rock. Lines were etched around his eyes, and she sensed they weren't caused by laughter but by harsher emotions. He studied her with a cool perusal.

Then he started to turn away from her. "I'm going to look in that saloon," he said.

Now. She had to make her move now.

Her heart pounded hard, and her throat was so dry she could barely breathe. She shifted and concentrated. She was good with a gun. As good as any man, Mac said. But he had taught her to shoot only for self-protection. In her heart, she knew he would not approve of this.

"One more step, and I'll kill you," she said.

He turned back to her.

"Go away," she tried one last time. "No one here but a few ghosts."

"And you." His dark gaze seemed to search her soul. "What's he to you?" He was trying to disarm her. She knew it, even as she realized it might be working. She widened her stance slightly and didn't bother to answer. Instead, her fingers inched closer to her holster. Don't stand there talking, Mac had taught her. Some gunmen will try to distract you with talk.

"Don't know what you mean."

"Why isn't he here? Why is he letting a kid protect him?"

She didn't reply. She had the terrible feeling that every time she did, she revealed more than she intended, that he saw under the disguise she'd so carefully assembled.

"I just want to take Thornton to trial. It will be fair."

"Not bloody likely."

He raised an eyebrow at that. "Then Thornton *is* here."

Blazes. She'd said too much.

She hadn't had much time to plan after a friend of Mac's from the old days had ridden in three hours earlier to warn him that a marshal named Evans was on the way. He'd moved on after issuing the warning. The man had a price on his head, as well.

Evans. She'd known that name. He'd been dogging Mac for years. A vendetta, Archie said once.

She tried to keep her hand from shaking as she stared into the marshal's eyes. She didn't want to kill him. Blazes, she didn't want to shoot him at all. But she could. She knew she could. She was fast. As fast as Mac had been in his heyday, and she'd beaten him to the draw more than once.

But this was no game between teacher and student.

The lawman took a step toward her, his arms at ease. He obviously didn't believe she would really draw.

Her heart quaked. If he reached her, he could easily disarm her. She was strong for a woman, but he was well over six feet and she suspected his lean body was all muscle.

Now.

"Draw!"

Her hand dove to the butt of her Colt. She saw a change in his eyes. He believed her now. His hand started toward his pistol, as well. A gust of hot wind caught her coat and flung the other side open.

Her finger pulled the trigger at the same second she realized his hand had stopped moving.

She heard the shot echo down the dirt road and saw the surprise in his eyes as his body buckled and he went down.

2

THE IMPACT of the bullet took Jared Evans by surprise.

Blood flowed from his right leg as it started to fold underneath him. The pain would follow. He knew that from too much experience. He prepared himself for it, even as he stared at the woman who had shot him.

In that split second as she went for the gun, the wind brushed open the coat and outlined the slim body. A woman. God damn, a woman. He'd been distracted just long enough...

He looked at her. She stood where she'd fired, gun firmly clutched in her hand.

He still held his gun as he fell to one knee. Instinct. *Never let go.* His fingers tightened around the grip. He tried to stand again, but his leg was deadweight. The dirt beneath him seemed to move, or was it him? He looked at his leg. Blood. Too much blood. An artery must have been hit.

He debated trying to return the shot. The woman still pointed her gun at him. He didn't know her intentions. She might come in for the kill. But he'd never shot a woman. He dropped the weapon and reached for the bandanna around his neck. *Tie off the leg....*

A woman, dammit....

The sun beat down on him as pain hit him. Sudden, searing pain ripped through his thigh as blood continued to flow from the wound and puddle on the ground. He finally tore the bandanna from his neck when he saw the shadow of the woman. If she shot again...

He looked up. She stood above him, her right hand still holding the Colt. He looked at his own gun. He *could* try to defend himself. But he'd seen enough wounds to know he didn't stand a chance if he didn't stop the bleeding. And his fingers didn't want to work....

She kicked his gun away and placed her own on the ground well out of his reach. Then she knelt beside him. She took the bandanna from his hands and without a word tied off his leg just above the wound and quickly twisted the cloth into a makeshift tourniquet. He noticed she did it expertly, as if she'd had more than a little practice.

"Hold that while I get something to keep it tight," she demanded.

He obeyed, even as the pain grew more intense. *Think of something else.* He concentrated on the woman's face, and his eyes met hers. Golden eyes. A light golden-brown, almost amber with flecks of gold. And the expression? Regret? Something more than that? An instant awareness flowed between them. Its power stunned him, left him dazed. *The wound.* It was the wound and the loss of blood.

But for an instant, her fingers froze on his leg. He knew from the intake of her breath she felt that odd pull, too. She hesitated, then breathed in deeply. Shaking her head slightly as if denying any reaction, she took a knife from a sheath on her gun belt and cut the trouser leg until she saw the wound.

He followed her glance. The bullet had driven cloth from his trousers into the flesh. He fought a wave of unconsciousness, even as he noticed her hands were callused. And gentle.

"The bullet's still inside," she said, confirming what he'd already suspected. Her voice trembled a bit, and he realized she wasn't as sure of herself as she tried to project. And her eyes weren't hard now. They were...worried.

For him?

Hard to believe.

He leaned on his arm, trying to muster his strength. He

wanted to pull her down to him and demand answers. She couldn't have been aiming for his leg; it would be far too dangerous. He could have killed her. And why was she now determined to help him? He tried to sit up but nothing was cooperating.

"Stay still," she said sharply.

He struggled to focus. The golden eyes were hard to read, and he was usually very good at judging people. Her hat was gone, and short tendrils of damp fawn-colored hair clung to her face, softening it. Pretty, he thought. How could he ever have taken her for a lad? Even for a moment.

He hurt too damn much to notice anything else. Neither was he in a position to question her help at the moment. The leg burned like hell, and he was fading.

"What the Sam Hill happened here?" Another shadow appeared in the late-afternoon sun. An old man sidled next to the woman and brushed her aside to examine the wound. Time had worn trails in his cheeks and forehead. A gray beard reached to the collar of his red shirt. He scowled as his rheumy eyes inspected the wound.

Jared tried to sit, but he fell back. He could barely keep his eyes open. How much blood had he lost in those few seconds?

"Damnation, girl, what did you go and do?" the old man asked.

Her face flushed. "He came for Mac," she said simply, as if that were answer enough.

"Mac ain't gonna like this," the old man said as if she hadn't spoken. He loosened the tourniquet, and the bleeding started again.

Jared wondered whether he meant the woman should have killed him. Or that he intended to do it himself.

"I'm a U.S. Marshal," he said. "The Denver sheriff knows where I was going. If I don't return, you'll have a posse up here."

"I'm real afeared," the old man said, as if swatting off a fly. He waited a few seconds after loosening the tourniquet, then tightened it again and muttered something indecipherable. He turned back to the woman. "Git some sheets and cut them into strips. Clean ones. Then hitch up Brandy. We can't leave the marshal here, and he's a big 'un. You and I will have to haul him to the saloon."

"The saloon?" the woman asked.

"Where else? Lessen you want to leave him to die out here?"

"But…" She stopped suddenly.

"This one ain't goin' nowhere for a while. Plenty of time to decide what to do with him. What did Mac tell you 'bout shooting? Make it good, or don't even think about it."

"I…I…"

If he didn't hurt so damn much and hadn't been the subject of the conversation, Jared would have been fascinated by the interplay between the old man and the girl. He supposed making it "good" meant killing him.

She left at a run, and the old man turned to him, grumbling as he did so. He studied the badge on Jared's shirt, then muttered an obscenity. "What's the name?" he finally asked.

"Jared…Evans." No use in denying it. Papers were in his pocket and saddlebags.

"Evans?" The man frowned. He apparently knew the name, but then many outlaws did. Jared traveled a lot, sent by territorial governors to wherever he was needed. No doubt any number of outlaws would like to see him dead.

Which might well include these two. He forced himself to a sitting position and felt the blood drain from his face. He glanced down at the knife he carried in his belt.

"Don't even think about it," the old man said as he eased the weapon out of its sheath. "Lessen you want to bleed to death." He paused, then asked, "Why are you here?"

The woman already knew why Jared was here. No sense in trying to lie. "Thornton. I have a warrant for him."

The old fellow's eyes sharpened. "I should leave you here to die."

"You a…a friend of his?" Jared was beginning to fade again.

Too many hours on horseback. Too little food. Now too little blood.

"Yeah, and I can tell you one thing. You ain't taking him."

"The…woman?"

"Sam? You don't need to know nothing about her, and you have to swear you'll forget you ever saw her if I fix you up."

"Can't…do that."

The old man stood. "Then you can bleed to death. Won't bother me none."

Jared knew he would do exactly that if he couldn't keep the tourniquet tight. He also knew he needed help. The bullet would have to come out. The wound would have to be cauterized. Even then he might well lose the leg to infection. Being a one-legged lawman didn't appeal much to him. Still, he wasn't going to lie, or violate his oath.

"Might matter to the…lady," he said harshly. "One thing to wound a lawman. Another to kill one."

The old man stood motionless for a moment, then sighed in surrender. "You know what we gotta do?"

"I know."

"You hurt her…I'll kill you. And if I don't, someone else will."

Jared didn't answer. He wasn't going to make promises he wouldn't keep. Not even to save his life.

The old man knelt again. This time Jared noted the stiffness in his movements. An old man and a young woman. They obviously knew MacDonald and where he was. Knew him well enough to kill for.

To die for.

SAM HURRIEDLY GRABBED a threadbare but clean sheet she'd washed yesterday. She stopped suddenly and leaned against a table. Her body started shaking. She'd almost killed a man. Maybe even had, if Archie couldn't control the bleeding. She would never forget the surprise on the marshal's face when he started to fall.

She closed her eyes and said a silent prayer. *Dear God, don't let him die.* She had wanted to stop him. Had to stop him. She hadn't thought beyond that.

His wound was serious, particularly with the cloth driven inside. And his leg? She didn't know how much damage she'd done to it. Could she have crippled him? Destroyed the pure masculine grace that had intrigued her?

She'd stopped him. She'd given Mac time. But she hadn't expected to feel this kind of remorse. A raw, wicked guilt that made her stomach turn. Maybe it was because he'd hesitated. He wasn't what she'd expected.

Neither had she expected the jolt that ran through her when their eyes met. Like a lightning strike. She still felt its heat inside her.

It was guilt. Nothing more.

Stop it! She'd done what she had to do, and now she was wasting time. She started tearing the sheet into strips. She heard Dawg yowl in the storeroom, but he would have to wait.

Damn the lawman. He *would* have to come now, just as she hoped they could finally head north. The four of them. An odd family at best. Archie and Mac and Reese. Her godfathers, as they jokingly called themselves. All three men had sacrificed for her. Each so different in looks and personal quirks, but ever so dear to her. Mac, the taciturn gunman; Reese, the handsome, easygoing gambler; and Archie, the curmudgeon. Mac was like her father, Archie like a grandfather, and Reese a charming uncle. They were the only family she'd known for the last ten years. She didn't aim to lose them.

She finished tearing the sheet. They would need a lot of bandages. The lawman's leg had bled copiously. Bone and muscles were probably damaged. Doctoring his wound was beyond her skills but not Archie's. He'd been a doctor's orderly during the Mexican American War.

He was also the closest thing to a doc this place ever had. When Gideon's Hope had been a roaring, lawless boom town, he was often called in the middle of the night to set a bone or sew up someone, even to birth a baby. After turning fifteen, she'd often gone along with him and helped.

Don't let there be permanent damage, she prayed. She would never forgive herself if there was, even if the lawman was a threat to the man who'd raised her, protected her, loved her like she was his own.

She gathered up several of the strips and hurried downstairs, her heart pounding every step. She kept seeing the marshal's face, startled at first, then clenched as the pain hit. Pain she'd inflicted. She bit hard on her lip.

Sam tried to dismiss the thought. *Mac's all that's important now.* She only wanted time for him to heal well enough so they could all go to Montana. They'd talked about building a ranch there someday. Reese had been to Montana and described it in vivid terms: rich grasslands, clear rivers and an endless sky. But it had always been *someday.* Something had always stopped them. Like not having enough money, or hearing talk of Indian troubles there, or Reese being away on one of his trips through the gold camps.

Why now? Why did the dratted marshal have to come now when they were almost ready. Another month and they would have been gone. Frustrated and still tormented by guilt, she raced out into the street. She handed the torn pieces of cloth to Archie.

"Get Brandy now," Archie said. "Sooner we get him out of this dirt, the better. Best we drive to the back of the saloon. It's only a few steps, then."

She didn't question him. A quick glance at the lawman made it evident he was in excruciating pain. Dammit, but those midnight-blue eyes would haunt her forever.

In another five minutes she had Brandy—Archie's old mule—hitched to the wagon and drove him out to the street.

The lawman was sitting up, but the effort was costing him. She saw that right away. His leg was straight out, a bandage wrapped tight around his thigh. The rest of his leg was bare. The soft material contrasted with the sheer masculinity of his powerful muscles.

His eyes were steady on her. He had a day's growth of beard but it didn't cover a slight scar on the left side of his face.

Sensuous lips had thinned in pain, and a muscle throbbed in his neck. He was a striking man, compelling in a stark way. His face was hard, but that harshness was broken by the barest hint of a dimple in his chin. And those damned dark eyes. Probing. Always probing.

That unfamiliar flicker of heat ran through her again.

"Come on, Sam," Archie said impatiently. "You're gonna have to help me lift him."

She leaned down, picked up her gun and started to replace it in her holster, then stopped as Archie frowned. "Empty your gun."

"He can't…"

Archie's expression made her do as he asked. Removing the remaining bullets, she tucked them in a pocket. Then she knelt and put one arm around the marshal. Archie did the same on the other side.

The marshal tried to help. But he was nearly a deadweight and he probably weighed more than she and Archie together. She was strong, though, and so was Archie, despite the rheumatism plaguing him. With their help, the marshal stood on one leg and slid onto the back of the wagon.

The white bandage was red now. The lawman's face was pale. She touched his cheek. It was damp with sweat. She sat next to him, trying to protect him from the bouncing that was to come.

"Go," she told Archie.

Archie didn't bother to get up on the bench. Instead he led old Brandy down the street to the corner, then around to the back of the saloon. With every bump, the marshal clenched his fingers into a fist, but he didn't utter a sound.

She knew what was to come would be worse. Much worse.

She wanted to touch him and somehow make his suffering more tolerable. But she couldn't. She couldn't take the shooting back and she knew she would never forget this day, this hour, these terrible minutes.

Maybe she should say a small prayer. But she didn't know any. Preachers hadn't lasted long in Gideon's Hope. Neither had teachers. All she knew was what her godfathers taught her and what she'd read in books.

She reminded herself that the marshal probably would have killed Mac. But that didn't help at the moment, nor did the thought that he hadn't shot her when he could have....

3

JARED TRIED to help as they dragged him inside what once must have been a busy saloon. But whenever he put any weight on his injured leg, new waves of agony coursed through him.

He ground his teeth to keep an expletive—or worse, a groan—from escaping his lips. He swayed as they entered the building. He tried to take a step with his good leg and sagged against the woman. Her arm tightened around his body. Stronger...than she looked. Hell...of a lot stronger.

A step, a hop.

He fought the fog closing in on him. Too much blood lost in those seconds before the tourniquet was in place. And the worst was yet to come. The damn bullet in his leg had to come out. He also knew the wound would probably need to be cauterized to stop the bleeding and infection.

He was only too aware that more men died in the Civil War from infections and fever than from ordnance. He'd been lucky thus far. He had survived three bullets: two during the war, one while marshaling. Shoulder. Side. Left arm. A bayonet had nicked his face.

He tried to focus on the woman rather than the pain. Who in the hell was she? Thornton's woman? Must be, to risk her life. Hell, the man must be decades older than she was.

Another step. Why? Why was he being helped inside? As a hostage maybe? To wait for Thornton? The original question pressed him: Why not just a bullet in his heart? Or had she really aimed for his leg? If so, it had been one hell of a gamble.

He might have made the same gamble, though. He was tired of killing. During those few tense minutes outside while he'd tried to avoid a shooting, his mind flickered back to a boy he'd encountered two months earlier. The kid was no more than seventeen, but Jared hadn't known that then. He'd only seen the gun in the boy's hand when Jared stepped out of the stable after feeding his horse.

He groaned inwardly, but it was more from the memory than pain. Why now, dammit? Why did those images continue to haunt him? Maybe he should have quit hunting men. He'd been at it far too long....

Then they were inside the saloon.

"Back room," the old man said to the girl, then as an aside to Jared, "Used it as a cell after the jail burned down."

Ironic.

The old man and the woman helped him through the back door of the saloon, then down the hall to a door. The woman opened it, and they half carried, half dragged him to an old iron bed and lowered him down on a thin, lumpy mattress. He made himself glance around the room. One chair and a small table in addition to the bed. Nothing else. Stout door. No windows.

His breathing was labored. The last of his strength was ebbing. So, apparently, was the old man's. His captor collapsed on the chair, his breath coming in spurts. But the woman...

She stood straight as if his weight hadn't been anything. Tall and slender...she was far stronger than she looked. Her gaze didn't waver as she met his. It was almost as if she was challenging that connection he'd felt a few minutes earlier. But it was there. He'd felt it, dammit. Felt it still. How could that be? Hellions had never appealed to him. Nor had women who chose the other side of the law.

He had little doubt she was Thornton's woman. Why else would she risk her life for him?

And why should he care whether she was or wasn't? Maybe because of the regret in those wide golden eyes as she looked at his wound. Or the gentleness in hands that seconds earlier had fired a gun. Or maybe the glimpse of vulnerability in her expression when the old man appeared.

Her cheeks started to flush as if she knew what he was thinking, or maybe it was because of what she was thinking. She turned abruptly, put a hand on the old man's back. "I'll get your bag and some water." She left the room in a quick stride. Straight. Proud. Defiant.

He fixed his thoughts on her. It blocked the pain, the knowledge of what he had to face next. Damn, but she intrigued him even now.

When she returned several minutes later, she had several sheets folded over her shoulder. She carried a black bag in one hand and a bowl of water in the other.

"Archie, are you all right?" Her voice softened as she placed the items on the table and knelt before the older man. Jared watched affection flicker between the two, and a pang of loneliness ran through him. He couldn't remember when someone had last worried about him.

"Stop fussin'," the man named Archie said. "Jest a mite winded. I'm all right now. Let's get started on him."

"I fired the stove and more water is heating. I'll bring it as soon as it's ready." She obviously knew what was needed. Jared remembered the deftness with which she'd taken over the tourniquet. He would bet that this wasn't the first time she'd treated a wounded man.

He was even more certain when she started to pull instruments from the bag and line them up on the table she placed next to the bed. He gritted his teeth as the old man yanked off his boots, then what was left of his pants. He cut away the right leg of Jared's long underwear but managed to leave enough fabric to cover his privates. Some shred of dignity at least.

Archie's ministrations weren't gentle, but they were efficient, and Jared was in no position to complain. He was totally at their mercy and that galled him. He knew the pain to come would be many times worse than their jostling.

"You a doctor?" Jared asked.

"Nope, but I've done some doctoring 'round these parts." Archie peered at the wound through a pair of spectacles he'd taken from a shirt pocket. "Have to take out the bullet and those scraps of cloth. I'll sew it if I can. Cauterize it if I can't. It'll hurt like the blazes, but from some of them scars, I 'spect you know that." He didn't sound very concerned.

Jared merely nodded. He'd been through this before.

"We have a small bit of laudanum," Archie said. "Maybe enough to help dull the pain."

Jared didn't like the idea of losing what little control he had. He damn well wanted to know what the man was doing to his leg. "Whiskey will do if you have some."

Archie shrugged. "Sam will get a bottle," he said, and the woman hurried from the room.

Sam? The old man had mentioned the name several times. Hell of a name for a woman. Even one who strapped on a gun and shot lawmen.

Archie put his hands in the bowl of water. Jared noticed the white foam. Soap. Good sign.

The man loosened the tourniquet again for a few seconds before retying it quickly. Despite the new rush of blood, Jared was grateful. Keeping the tourniquet tight would cut off the blood supply to the lower leg and he could lose it. He tried to sit upright to see what was going on, but he fell back, his breath ragged. God, he was weak.

He gritted his teeth as the old man chose a probe from the instruments the woman had lined up.

Concentrate on something else. "I would like to know the name of the man cutting me," he said. "And…the lady's."

His captor frowned at him, obviously taking exception to the way he referred to the woman. "Since you ain't likely to spread it anytime soon," the old man said, "might as well tell you. I'm Archibald Smith. Archie to my friends. Smith to you. And the lady, she's just Sam."

Jared tried to wrap his mind around that. He couldn't. She might be a lot of things, but she certainly wasn't "just Sam."

"Your daughter?"

"Nah."

The old man was stingy with information. Jared clenched his teeth as he probed around the wound. Christ, it already felt as if someone was sticking white-hot knives in him. "You... raised her?"

Archie sat back and studied him with pale, watery eyes. "Sam pretty much raised herself." He hesitated, then added, "Heard of you. Didn't much like what I heard."

"Because I'm a lawman?"

"You've been hunting Mac for years. That ain't just marshaling, that's something else. Something dark."

The probe went deeper, and Jared's fingers knotted in fists. After a second, he asked, "Then why are you taking the bullet out? You could have left me..."

"Could've, but Mac wouldn't have liked it. He wouldn't want Sam to kill anyone." The old man shook his head. "Me, I'm not sure it would be a bad thing."

Mac again. Jared tried to concentrate on the man's words. *Mac wouldn't want Sam to kill anyone.*

Mac must be Thornton, who also went by MacDonald. Maybe they knew Thornton would want to get rid of Jared himself. The old man just admitted they knew he had been trailing the outlaw for years. He wanted to ask more, but then Archie poked the wound again. Jared's body arched involuntarily, and the room began to fade in and out.

"If you know what's good for you, you'll forget about Sam." The old man spoke softly, but there was no mistaking the warning. "No one messes with her and lives."

It seemed to Jared that it had been Sam doing the messing, but he didn't reply, partly for fear it might come out as a groan. The pain was too intense. His body shivered. He tried to lie still, tried to adapt to the ever increasing waves of agony. There would be more. Maybe he should have taken the laudanum.

Archie muttered something Jared couldn't decipher. He tried to concentrate on the words. His life might depend on it. Thornton. MacDonald. A killer with a price on his head. Yet this old man and the woman—Sam—talked about him as if he were some kind of god.

Then Sam returned again, this time holding a bottle of whiskey topped by a cup in one hand, a second bowl of steaming water in the other. She placed the water on the table, then filled the cup with whiskey. She lifted his head as she put the cup to his lips. "Drink," she ordered.

Knowing what was coming, he gulped down several swallows. He still didn't know what skill Smith had, but he did know the bullet could eventually kill him if it weren't removed.

He stared up at the woman. His eyesight was blurring. She didn't seem boyish now with soft hair framing her face. More... like an angel.

An angel who had shot him.

He finished off the strong, bitter whiskey.

She poured more, but he shook his head. Best to get this over with.

She placed the cup on the table, then dunked a piece of cloth into one of the bowls, took a deep breath and wiped the blood from around the wound. The cloth was hot, burning, but he was grateful for it. The heat would increase his chances of survival, of preventing infection.

There was a stillness in her face, like a mask, as if she were afraid to show any emotion. Only a flicker of her tongue against her lips gave her away. A tendril of hair fell over her forehead and he caught the scent of roses.

Sarah had smelled of roses, too.

Archie probed deeper.

Jared sucked in a deep breath. *Christ.* He needed something to bite on. Almost as if she read his mind, she stuck a piece of wood between his teeth. He crunched down on it, waiting for the worst of the pain to subside. Then Archie stopped fishing around.

He felt the wet cloth against the tender skin again and looked back at the woman. Damn, why did she have to be...pretty? And dangerous? She'd done what few men had: bested him in a gunfight.

If he lived through this, he had to remember that. He suspected those golden eyes could make a man forget almost anything. When she finished cleaning the area around the wound, Archie gave him a long look. "I got most of the cloth out. The bullet's deep, lodged against the bone. We can tie your hands and feet to the posts. You don't wanta be moving when…"

Jared shook his head and dropped the wood from his mouth. "Get…on with…it."

The woman put the wood back in place, and he bit down as the probe reentered the wound. His left hand clutched the iron frame of the bed. Sam stood next to Archie, washing away blood as the old man worked. Spasms of fresh pain shot through Jared's thigh and up his body. His teeth chomped harder on the wood and he squeezed his fingers into tight fists. Waves of agony, each worse than the last, swept over him.

Then he was aware of her hand holding his, that he was gripping it. He opened his eyes and saw a tear halfway down her cheek. Her lips were bleeding from biting into them.

Maybe he was imagining it. Or maybe it was the whiskey. He closed his eyes again as the old man pulled out the bullet. *Remember. Remember the good times.*

Sarah. Sarah stood there in the door of their farmhouse, that grand smile spreading across her face….

THE MARSHAL'S BODY RELAXED. Sam's body eased, as well, as he lapsed into unconsciousness. She couldn't feel the full extent of his pain, but some part of it radiated into her. She'd done this to him.

Thank God, he was finally unconscious. It seemed like an hour but must have been no more than three or four minutes before Archie held up a bullet. "Got it," he said with satisfaction, and dropped it onto the table. Then he went in again and fished out more pieces of fabric. Concealing her bruised hand, she started swabbing the wound again with the wet cloth.

"How bad is it?" Sam asked.

"Bad enough. Lodged against a bone and tore some muscles. Be a while before he can walk again. But if it doesn't putrefy, he should be all right." He looked at the gaping wound. It still bled. "I have to cauterize it."

"You can't sew it?"

"It's bleeding pretty bad. Safer to sear it shut." He looked at her closely. "Best do it while he's out."

She retreated to the kitchen area and fetched the knife she'd left in the stove to heat. She stood by as Archie poured sulfur in the wound, then touched the white-hot blade to the marshal's skin. Shivers ran through her as the smell of burning flesh permeated the room. Thank God the man was still unconscious. But when he woke…

Archie looked weary, the lines in his face deeper than usual.

"You go see to Mac," she said. "I'll put some salve on the wound and look after him."

"Better change clothes first. You got blood all over you." Archie wearily walked to the door. "Damn fool shoulda taken the laudanum. Got guts, though." He sighed. "Don't know what in the hell we'll do with him. Might have been best to just let him bleed to death."

She didn't answer that. There was no answer. She hadn't planned ahead. She'd only thought about the immediate need to protect Mac.

As for courage? The marshal undoubtedly had that.

Sam took one last look at the unconscious man, then went to release Dawg from the storeroom, where she'd placed him before the confrontation in the street. He'd known something was different, and she hadn't wanted him to alert Archie or, worse, try to follow her.

The half mutt, half wolf regarded her quizzically when the door opened. Then he tentatively wagged his tail. She leaned down and petted him, assuring him all was well, even if it wasn't. Dawg cocked his head, trying to understand, then whined.

She'd found Dawg four years ago, his leg half torn off by an old trap. Archie had doctored him, and he'd chosen to stay with them.

He sniffed her now, apparently smelling the blood on her and the scent of a new person. He knew something was wrong but apparently no longer sensed immediate peril for those he cared about. He followed her up to her room and watched protectively as she put on a clean shirt and trousers.

When she finished, she hesitated, trying to steady herself. She'd always been independent. And strong. She'd helped her mother run a boardinghouse until her death when Sam was eleven. Her father had died several years earlier, and there had been no living relatives. Mac, Reese and Archie—all of whom had loved her mother—promised to care for Sam. One of them was usually gone, one was always in town, and each had taught her his special skills, and most of all, how to take care of herself.

She'd never questioned why they'd stayed here when everyone else left. To her, it made sense. Gideon's Hope was a safe place for Mac. Few people even realized it still existed after the gold ran out. They'd had some visitors. The hopeful who thought they might still strike it rich. Sometimes friends of Mac or Reese or Archie. But visitors were increasingly rare these past few years. The town had made a convenient base for Reese, who gambled up and down the gold camps and now the silver mines, and Mac and Archie both loved the mountains. They had a comfortable home in the saloon Reese owned. There were plenty of trout in the stream, game in the forest and enough remaining nuggets carried down by mountain rain to pay for any additional supplies they needed.

As for her schooling, she had three teachers. Reese had attended Cambridge University in England, and Mac the University of Virginia until the war started. Between the two, she'd learned to love knowledge. Reese had collected books from all over Colorado, and she'd read every one. He'd introduced her to Shakespeare and poets along with penny novels and romances. Mac was more interested in sums and astronomy because that was something he could use.

From Archie, she learned the greatest gift of all: healing. She'd begged Archie when she was no more than thirteen to take her along with him on one of his calls, and over the years he'd taught her more and more. Even when the last of the residents left, she continued to help him with mountain folks—and even some Indians—who'd heard of Archie and made their way to Gideon's Hope. And she'd helped him mend creatures who needed it.

At her request, Reese had brought her books on medicine and she'd built a small library. She sometimes dreamed about being a doctor, but she never told her godfathers. She knew it would mean leaving them and she was too indebted to them for that. Archie was slowly going blind, and Mac, well, what would Mac do without having to fret about her? The valley was the only safe place in Colorado for him.

The one thing they didn't teach her was how to be a woman, and for a long time she hadn't cared. After most of the miners and merchants left, she had a freedom she relished. She loved running barefoot in the summer and swimming nude in the mountain spring. She could ride like the wind and play a fine game of poker.

They had been talking, though, about going north to Montana, where Mac wouldn't be known. Starting a ranch with the money they'd saved from years of on-and-off panning for gold and Reese's winnings.

Her godfathers didn't have medicine in mind with the move. They wanted her to "have a more normal life." She knew exactly what they meant by that. The male species. She'd heard them talk about her future, how she "needed" to meet some men—prospective husbands. And, truth be told, she'd been feeling stirrings inside, a longing for something she couldn't quite define.

And there was no one to explain it to her.

But apparently Mac had sensed it. And for that reason, he'd left the safety of Gideon's Hope. He'd planned on trading in the nuggets they'd collected over past years for cash for the trip north. For her. Only for her.

If not for her, he wouldn't be lying upstairs as much dead as alive.

She decided to check on him. She wanted to reassure herself she'd done the right thing by shooting the marshal. She needed that mental weapon before she saw the wounded man again.

She went past the five empty rooms that had once been occupied by the women who worked below, and sometimes above. She'd known many of them, and they hadn't seemed soiled doves to her. After her mother died, they'd been kind to her, even taught her to play the guitar and to sing songs, both pretty and naughty.

Archie was hunched over Mac when she opened the door. "How is he?" she asked.

"Still slipping in and out," Archie said.

"He didn't hear anything?"

Archie simply shook his head.

She went over to the bed and looked down at the man who was the closest thing to a father she had. Father. Friend. Teacher. Confidante. Her heart lurched as she gazed at his wounded body. He'd arrived barely alive four days earlier, and must have used every remnant of strength he had to reach them. He'd been ambushed by bounty hunters. He thought he'd killed two and wounded a third, but the cost was high. He had two bullets in him and a third had smashed his right hand.

It had taken him nearly two days to reach Gideon's Hope, and by that time one of the wounds had festered. She and Archie had packed it with poultices made of moss, using old Indian remedies Archie had picked up over the years. They'd also gone through most of what little laudanum Archie had hoarded. The fever had lessened, but Mac still alternated between being unconscious and delirious. His breathing was labored and she knew he couldn't be moved again.

He had always been so strong and sure, so capable in every way. And now his right hand—his gun hand—was buried in a swath of bandages. His unruly sandy hair was touched with gray and his normally sun-bronzed face looked years older than forty-five. A sandy beard covered his cheeks and chin.

Still buffeted by emotions, she drew a deep breath. She *had* done the right thing, she told herself. The only thing. But what now? Two wounded men. What if the marshal recovered quickly and discovered Mac above him? What then? Her chest tightened.

She wished Reese was here with his cocky grin and quick hands and seemingly endless knowledge. He was close to Mac's age, but they couldn't be less alike. The third son of an English lord, Reese was destined to go into the church. Instead, he escaped to the West to make his own fortune, and he'd never been particular as to how he did it. Reese considered life one big joke while Mac was intense and quiet. They had been competitors while her mother lived, and friends after.

"I'll go look after the marshal," she said. She had to keep busy. Then maybe she wouldn't think.

With Dawg at her side, she picked up several more sheets from the room and went back downstairs. The lawman was still unconscious. The sheet Archie had placed under him was bloody, along with what was left of the long johns he wore. They no longer covered much of anything and she couldn't take her eyes from him. Her body suddenly reacted to his, and she took a deep breath. This had never happened before, but then Archie had always tried to block her from seeing that particular piece of anatomy.

Dawg inched in and bristled as if he detected danger.

"Friend," she told him softly. Dawg immediately backed off and sat several feet away.

The marshal was no friend, but she didn't want Dawg to inflict more damage on the man. She reminded herself he was the enemy. He hadn't had to come here. But he didn't look like an enemy now. He looked like someone who was suffering.

She angrily brushed away a tear at the edge of her eye. She'd done what she had to do. She kept telling herself that.

First things first. She took a bottle of salve from Archie's bag and liberally spread it over the wound. It would ease the pain and hopefully speed the recovery.

She fetched fresh water and washed his face where sweat had mingled with dirt, then took stock of every feature. Strong angular bones with thick black brows and eyelashes. The dimple in his chin barely dented the hard face. His cheekbones were lightly covered with new bristles of beard, and his dark hair was matted with sweat, a hank of it falling over his forehead.

Not exactly handsome but intriguing. For a moment he fit the image she had of Heathcliff from *Wuthering Heights,* one of the many books Reese had found for her. Dark and dangerous. But, unlike Heathcliff, she sensed there was little recklessness in this man. The intensity was there, though. She'd seen it in his eyes.

She also remembered the story had a very unsatisfactory ending and tried to dismiss it from her mind.

Instead she took inventory. The area around the wound was clean, but he was filthy from the dust, the blood and the sweat.

The shirt had to come off. It was soaked. She didn't think she could pull it off, though, without waking him. She decided to cut it away. Mac was about the same size and had several shirts. The marshal could use one of those.

Archie had taken his medical bag with him but he'd left the marshal's knife on the table. A sudden chill went through her. It was unlike Archie to be careless. She would have to watch him more carefully.

She turned her attention back to her patient. She cut off the sleeves of the shirt, then attacked the problem of the sheets. She rolled him as far as she could, taking the bloody sheet with him, then placed a fresh one on the bed. She rolled him back onto the other side, careful of his leg, and was able to pull off his shirt and the soiled sheet, leaving the clean one under him. With a deep breath, she took stock of the chore ahead.

His chest was solid muscle, brown and dusted with dark hair that arrowed down to his abdomen. She'd helped Archie doctor before and was no stranger to most of a man's body. But definitely never one this fine. Taken as a whole, he was magnificent. *Sinewy.* Reese had taught her that word, but she'd never entirely grasped the meaning until now.

Thank God he was unconscious. She couldn't let him see that she was affected by him.

She shook her head. A moment of foolishness.

She rinsed and soaped her cloth and skimmed it over his shoulders and across his chest. Placing the cloth back in the water, she felt his skin. Smooth and warm and covered with soft, springy body hair. Unexpectedly soft. She swallowed. Everything else was so hard.

She drew the cloth across the patterned ridges of his chest and found herself moving it down toward his stomach legs and what little was left of his long johns.

She was twenty—nearly twenty-one—and had never been with a man in a sexual way. Stolen kisses, yes. A few dances with boys when she was fifteen, before the fire that destroyed most of the town and caused most of the residents to flee. But never more than a kiss. One reason was her protectors. No man, young or old, wanted to go up against Mac or Reese, or even Archie with his wicked whip. Her godfathers had made it real clear in the rough mining town they would kill anyone who trifled with her.

She knew all about nature, though. She'd seen her share of cows and horses mate. Goats and dogs, too. Hadn't seemed all that great to her. As for humans, she'd seen the sadness of the soiled doves who'd once served the miners of Gideon's Hope. Their relationships with men were nothing like the romances she'd read about in the novels Reese brought her. Nothing like the wild, runaway passion of Emily Brontë's characters.

Her skin had never tingled, nor had she experienced a deep yearning inside. Until now. She looked down at the marshal and felt an inexplicable rush of heat. Maybe her skin wasn't tingling, but something was happening inside as she ran the cloth across his stomach.

Her throat suddenly tightened as that warmth puddled in the core of her. An intense need clutched at her. She didn't know exactly what she was feeling. She just knew it was there. Hungry and wanting.

He's the enemy.

That reminder did nothing to ease the bubbling cauldron that was her stomach. Nor did it make breathing easier.

She forced her gaze away from his flat abdomen and finished washing him as best she could. She couldn't help but notice the scars on his body. One on his shoulder, and another on his side. A scar along his hairline was nearly hidden by the thick, dark hair.

He would have another one now. Large and ugly. Because of her.

She lightly bandaged his wound, then arranged another fresh sheet over him. He moved then, thrashed, and muttered something. A name she couldn't quite make out. A cry of anguish.

She stilled. Then she put her arms around him to keep him from sliding off the bed and hurting his leg more. Empathy flowed through her. Something inside him hurt every bit as wickedly as the wound. Guilt mixed with the other confusing feelings. She didn't like pain inflicted on man or beast, but she'd had no other choice. She kept telling herself that.

There's always choices. Mac's words. He'd made all the wrong ones, he told her once after he'd had some drinks.

Mac and Reese and Archie. Her world. Her family. Her only family. And this man threatened one of them. Maybe all of them.

Yet the marshal had had a chance to shoot, and he'd hesitated.

He quieted now and his breathing eased. She stood. She had to leave for a few moments before guilt—and that intense need—suffocated her. Water. He would need fresh water when he woke.

When she returned with a full pitcher, Dawg was still sitting near the door. The marshal groaned, and his eyes flickered open. As if he sensed her presence, he turned his pain-filled gaze toward her. Like a hawk with a broken wing. Predatory and fierce even while crippled.

"Water or whiskey?" she asked, trying to keep her tone even, trying not to think about the past half hour.

"Water." His voice was flat, but his eyes were bloodshot and the lines around them deep with suffering.

She raised his head and held it up while he gulped down the

contents of the cup she'd filled. When he finished she lowered him back to the bed. He tried to raise himself. His face paled, and he clutched the side of the bed.

"Don't move," she ordered. "We didn't go to all that trouble to see you ruined again."

"Why *did* you go to that trouble?"

She shrugged, tried to hide the emotions flooding her. The warmth of his skin lingered on hers. And now she felt that tingling again, and it was unlike any sensation she'd ever known. She swallowed hard. She wanted to touch him again, wanted to know more of those feelings. Instead, she tried to banish them. It was a betrayal of Mac. Of herself. "Wouldn't watch a varmint die in the street." She hoped her voice wasn't as husky as she feared.

Dawg whined from behind her, nudged her.

"He's...wanted," the marshal said, his voice ragged. "There are others looking..."

"Not you, for a while," she retorted.

A muscle jerked in his cheek. His eyes closed for a moment, then opened. His gaze was intense, as if he was looking through to her soul, and a shiver ran down her back.

Dawg brushed by her. He placed his big head on the bed and growled. He sensed conflict, and he didn't like it.

The marshal's eyes went to the dog. "Who...is that?"

"Dawg," she replied, and for the briefest of moments she thought she might have seen a flash of humor.

He went up a notch in her estimation. He hadn't asked what but who. Dawg usually intimidated everyone he met. He was big and considered ugly by most. But to her he was intensely loyal and brave.

Now he inspected the wounded marshal more closely, baring his teeth as he usually did with strangers.

The marshal stared back at him. Not the slightest flinch. Everyone flinched when they first saw Dawg. Then he said something so softly that she couldn't make it out.

Dawg inexplicably relaxed. Made a funny noise in his throat. Blue blazes, an accepting noise.

Perplexed, she studied the man in the bed. "He's not real fond of strangers," she warned.

"Neither...are you," he observed. "Apparently...it's epidemic in Gideon's Hope." His mouth twisted in a wry smile.

The marshal's body suddenly seized again, and his lips clamped down. She found the bottle of whiskey she'd used earlier and quickly filled the cup he'd just emptied. She had to hold his head up again as he drank. When he finished, he turned his gaze to Dawg, trying, she figured, to distract himself from the pain. "Dawg?" His voice was ragged.

"I found him when he was little more than a pup," Sam continued. "He'd been abandoned and got caught in a beaver trap. Archie saved his paw. Archie always called him the danged dawg. Then everyone did."

"And me... What do you plan...now?" Every word seemed an effort, but she knew what he was asking.

"I don't know," she said honestly. "I didn't think that far ahead."

The side of his lips turned up in a wry half smile, as if he were surprised by her admission.

She was surprised, too. She hadn't meant to show that vulnerability.

The words had just popped out when he fixed his dark eyes on her.

"You ever shoot anyone before?" he asked suddenly.

But before she could figure how to answer, she saw him tense in pain. The cauterized leg must be agonizing. Sweat covered his brow. She quickly filled the cup again. His fingers reached for it and touched hers. Heat flowed from him to her. Their eyes met, engaged in a silent but oddly intimate battle. Every bone and nerve in her body was excruciatingly aware of him.

She was so startled she nearly dropped the cup, and he was the one who steadied it. He took a few sips, then sank back against the rough pillow.

Had he felt that same awareness? Or was it only her imagination, stirred by books?

Flustered, she shifted her feet. "I'll look after your horse. You should get as much sleep as…"

As someone she'd just shot could.

4

WHAT WAS HAPPENING to her?

Tremors were running up and down her spine as she left the room. And her breathing? It was coming in short little blasts.

She should be afraid of the marshal, of what he could do. But what frightened her even more was something other than fear. It was the unexpected longing that clawed at her, striking a wild, lonely chord deep inside.

The constriction in her chest grew tighter. She didn't want to be anyone's enemy. Especially his, a secret voice whispered.

Sam took a deep breath. Think of something else. Anything else.

The marshal's horse, she reminded herself. Animals always soothed her, and the horse probably needed water and feed.

The roan waited in front of the livery.

She concentrated on the animal. Archie and Mac had both told her you could tell a lot about a man by the way he treated his horse, and she knew immediately this one had been treated well. She remembered how the marshal had said only a soft word and Dawg had practically slobbered all over him. She'd never seen the animal do anything like that before.

But the marshal was a hunter. A hunter of men. And, from everything she'd heard, a ruthless one.

She went over all his words, then stopped as she recalled one fevered utterance. "There will be others."

A shiver of fear ran down her back as she grabbed the horse's reins and led him inside the stable.

Burley met her at the door.

"Is he dead?" Burley asked.

"No. If anyone else comes looking for the marshal or Mac, you haven't seen them." Her eyes bored into Burley and she tried to make her voice as coldly resolute as Mac's. "Understand? Because if you don't, Archie will take his whip to you."

From the way his eyes widened at the last threat, Burley obviously had more respect for Archie's wrath than her own.

"Didn't mean to tell him nothin', Sam," he groveled. "Honest."

She felt a second of guilt. Burley had dived into a bottle years ago after he lost his claim in a poker game. She had no idea how old he was, but he stayed in Gideon's Hope because she and Mac and Archie looked out for him. Although his help wasn't needed, he cared for the animals in return for food and an occasional drink of whiskey. Burley had pride.

"You told him where Mac was," she accused.

"No, I swear. He came in and asked 'bout feed for his horse. When he saw Mac's pinto, he asked about buying it. I said he wouldn't be for sale, that Mac thought he was something special. That's all I said. I swear."

"You mentioned Mac's name?"

He hung his head.

She sighed.

Probably didn't make any difference, anyway. The marshal evidently knew that Mac rode a pinto and, even worse, had discovered where Mac was hiding. She took pity on Burley. "Maybe you should put Mac's horse in the last stall."

"He gonna live? That lawman?"

She nodded. "He lost a lot of blood, but Archie worked on him."

"You shot him," Burley said admiringly.

She didn't reply right away. The agony on the marshal's face as Archie dug for the bullet flashed in her mind. "Rub his horse down and give him some oats."

He nodded, eager to redeem himself. "I've been saving some," he said. "Mr. Reese...he said he would be bringing more." He looked at her wistfully. "You think he'll be back soon?"

Sam fervently hoped so. She and Mac and Archie never knew when Reese would return from his travels. If he was on a winning streak, it could be several more weeks. He knew, though, that Mac wanted to leave for Montana as soon as possible. Now they would have to wait until he was stronger.

She had been the one who kept looking for delays. Her mother and father were buried here and she couldn't imagine life anywhere else.

But now was time to give back. Archie needed her. So did Mac. He was no longer safe here. Maybe never had been. Maybe one of his old outlaw friends had gotten drunk and said something. Or, more likely, he'd been recognized while in Denver. If only the marshal hadn't kept the hunt alive. Maybe then everyone would have forgotten about Mac.

She remembered his long strides when he returned from a trip, the way he took steps two at a time to see her mother. She'd seen the joy on her mother's face when he arrived after a long absence, but she also remembered the arguments they'd had when she was a child. He wouldn't marry her because of the price on his head. When her mother died of pneumonia, he and Archie and Reese had sworn to take care of her. Mac, though, had been the one closest to her. He was the one who wiped her tears, taught her to ride and protected her.

Then, months ago, Reese had suggested Montana as a possibility to give Sam "more opportunities." He'd been there years earlier and talked grandly about the land. It didn't hurt that there were numerous mining communities to be picked, as well. But until recently, the Sioux and Blackfeet had both been active in the territory. Now that the army was conducting a major campaign against them, he felt this was the time to go. Land was available under the Homestead Act, and it could be supplemented by open range to graze cattle.

Sam didn't care about the kind of "opportunities" her

godfathers were considering. Marriage was what they meant, and she wasn't sure that's what she wanted. Surely a husband would expect her to be like other wives. He would frown on her riding astride and helping Archie doctor folks. She wasn't reassured by any marriages she'd seen in Gideon's Hope. Worn women who looked decades older than their real ages waited at home with multiple children while their husbands drank and gambled what little money they had. Hadn't her mother done just fine on her own after Sam's father died?

But maybe, just maybe, Sam could learn more about medicine. The farther Mac was from Colorado, the safer he would be.

She had dropped her objections then, and they made plans. Reese would take one last round of the mining camps to raise money. She would can the early vegetables they'd grown in the garden. Mac would bring in game and they would smoke it, and Archie would take what gold they'd panned to Denver and get cash for it. They would need it to buy cattle along the way.

But Archie was beset with rheumatism, and Mac had become restless. He didn't think anyone would recognize him. He'd grown a beard, and the trip to Denver would be in and out.

Someone did recognize him, though, and now the marshal threatened everyone she loved. Mac. Archie. Even Reese, who'd been harboring Mac all these years.

She led the marshal's roan into the stall. Burley fetched a bucket of water from the well in back, and together they gave him fresh hay.

"I'll unsaddle and rub him down," Burley said, eager to make amends.

She took the marshal's saddlebags and bedroll, then stood back. Maybe there would be some clothes in them. She didn't want to keep seeing his nakedness. It was bad enough that the image lingered in her thoughts. She didn't like the heat that drove through her when it did.

Nor the churning in her stomach when he looked at her with those cool, dark blue eyes.

HAD HE IMAGINED a gentle hand touching him? Even caressing him?

Cool. It had been a brief moment of relief in his fevered world. Soothing.

Sarah? He'd thought that for a moment, then remembered. Sarah was gone. Had been gone for years.

Jared slipped in and out of consciousness. He preferred the darkness to the fire racing through his leg. When he was conscious, he tried to think of anything but the pain.

The woman. Think of the woman! Must have been her hands he'd felt. He had to learn more about her, and her relationship to the man she called Mac.

His life depended on it. Maybe she hadn't intended to kill him, but from everything he'd heard about MacDonald, he couldn't count on the same from the outlaw.

He tried to remember what she and the old man said about MacDonald, but the words slipped in and out of his memory. Nothing he'd heard, though, fit the image of the man he was hunting.

The poster had been in his pocket. Probably a bloody mess now, but he'd been tracking the man on and off for nearly ten years. The man she called MacDonald had been named Thornton when he took part in the stagecoach robbery. Jared had confirmed that when he caught one of the men who'd robbed the coach. The man claimed Thornton was the one who'd shot and killed Emma. He'd hung anyway.

He'd tracked the man for six months, then lost the trail, although Thornton had never been far from his thoughts. Occasionally over the years he would get a lead, but it never panned out. Someone had thought he'd seen Thornton in a mining town in central Colorado, but that was years ago. Then he'd heard that Thornton had changed his name to MacDonald. Finally, a week ago, a young would-be gun hand heard someone say a wanted outlaw was spotted in Denver. He gathered two friends and went after him. Only one of the three returned.

It was enough to give Jared a head start. He'd heard that the young gun hand's father was hiring men to avenge his son's death. He didn't think the others knew exactly where Thornton was hiding, but they would figure it out.

Now he was damned close to the man and couldn't do a blasted thing about it. Not at the moment anyway.

Why was a woman living in a nearly deserted ghost town some seventy miles away from the nearest civilization? Young and...intriguing, even in a man's garb. Had to be Thornton's mistress. An outlaw's mistress. A killer's woman. Or was she simply an outlaw herself? Part of Thornton's band?

Sam raised herself. The old man had used his words sparingly.

But now she was full grown. Without the coat, it was obvious that she'd reached womanhood. Her breasts pressed against her shirt, and there was a long-legged grace in her movements. And her eyes. God, they were remarkable. He wondered how she would look in a dress.

He tried not to think about the jolt of awareness that had shot between them in the street despite his pain. Nor did he wish to think about the gentleness of her fingers when she was assisting the old man. Efficient but gentle. It was obvious that she had tended wounds before.

An odd combination for an outlaw. Or an outlaw's woman.

He moved slightly. The pain was so excruciating that he wanted to sink back into oblivion. He looked down at his bandaged thigh. The wound felt hot and angry and burned like the furies from hell. The barest movement sent fresh frissons of agony through him.

He tried to ignore it. He glanced around the small room. The door was closed. His gun? Neither it nor his holster was in sight. A bowl sat on the table, along with a pitcher and cup. Nothing else.

His throat was parched. He reached for the water, but it was beyond him. With a massive effort he tried to move his legs from the bed to the floor, and the room started to swim. *Will.* All it would take was will.

He lowered his legs to the floor, his teeth clenched to keep from crying out. He was so damned weak. A step. Just a step. *Water.*

He stood, wavered, then crashed down, his body hitting the bed and knocking over the table. Then everything went black again.

SAM LEFT Burley unsaddling the horse and carried the marshal's possessions to the saloon. She thought about opening the door and checking on him, but she hadn't been gone that long and she wasn't sure she was up to another encounter with him. She didn't fear him, but she was wary of the way she reacted to him.

Instead, she put the saddlebags and bedroll on a table and opened the bedroll first. She wasn't spying, she assured herself. He needed some clean clothes after all.

A heavy jacket fell out, along with a rain slicker. Then she looked through the saddlebags. A pair of leg and wrist manacles. They felt hard and cold and ugly in her hands. She carefully placed them on the table and continued looking. There was a pair of pants, an extra shirt, socks and one set of clean underwear. A container of matches wrapped in oilskin. Then she found a well-worn book by someone named Victor Hugo.

Books were precious to her. She looked at the title. Reese had never mentioned this one. She put it down and continued her search. Some hardtack and coffee. No photographs or miniatures. No other personal items.

She folded the clothes and put the manacles back in the saddlebags. They might just need the latter.

Archie would be up with Mac, just as he had been these past few days. The two usually argued constantly, but they were close friends, and she knew Mac probably would have died had Archie not pushed him into living. And kept pushing.

She sat down at the table and closed her eyes. Everything hit her then. She had nearly killed a man. If the marshal died of blood poisoning, she would have succeeded. Now she knew what Mac meant about killing. A target was one thing, but a man...that was something else.

What if he died?

She shouldn't care. But hell's blazes, she did. He had grit for sure. Any other man would have been screaming when Archie poked around for the bullet, then pressed the white-hot knife against the wound.

And something…something had passed between them for the briefest second as she was cleaning the wound, when his gaze met hers. An awareness that had nothing to do with the fact she'd shot him. It had been like a lightning bolt—and a remnant still burned inside her.

Dawg came over, rested his big head in her lap and whined in sympathy. She leaned down and put her arms around him, soaking in the comfort he was offering.

A crash jerked her back to the moment. Dawg's ears pricked and he ran to the back room.

She hurried after him and opened the door. She hadn't locked it, thinking the marshal was far too weak to move. Anyone else would still be unconscious.

He lay sprawled on the floor. It was obvious he'd tried to stand. Darn fool. His leg was bleeding again. Blood spread across the bandage.

She heard a noise behind her and spun around. Archie was in the doorway.

"What happened?" he asked.

"He must have tried to get up."

"More trouble than he's worth," Archie mumbled.

She couldn't have agreed more. Yet there was something about the man—the uncompromising set of his mouth, the hank of dark hair that fell over his forehead.

He was unconscious. And naked except for a scrap of bloody long johns.

Archie took one of his arms and she took the other. Together they got him back on the bed. She quickly pulled the sheet over his near-nakedness.

She averted her eyes, but she couldn't stop the warmth creeping up her neck. And other places. *It's just the summer heat.* It had been warm all day and was particularly so in the small, windowless room.

"Maybe he needed water," she said.

"Damn fool shoulda waited."

Archie unwrapped the bandage from his leg and frowned. The burn looked wicked and blood seeped around it. He muttered about wasted effort and damn fools.

"I'll make a poultice," Sam said.

Archie rewrapped the marshal's leg.

He signaled her to go outside. He followed and closed the door behind him. "Best make it two," he said.

"Is Mac worse?" she asked.

"He ain't no better. He's having those nightmares again. Someone has to be with him all the time or he might start thrashing about and hurting hisself again. I don't even want to be gone now, but I heard the crash. You gonna have to see to the marshal yourself." He paused and looked at the saddlebags on the table. "Anything in 'em?"

"A shirt and a pair of trousers. Undershirt. Wrist and leg irons. A book."

"Get that shirt on 'im. And keep him covered with that sheet. Don't like him being so naked."

"I've seen men before," she said. "You let me help you doctor them."

"Mebbe so, but that was then and this is now," he said grumpily, and looked at Dawg, who was at her heels. "And take Dawg with you. Hound ain't good for nothing 'cept looking after you."

She nodded. She didn't tell Archie that Dawg had already made an overture to the marshal. It wouldn't sit well at all.

"Manacles may come in handy," Archie continued. "He ain't going no place now, but we might need them later. He seems like a mighty determined man." His frown deepened. "I don't like leaving you with him but Mac needs me. You watch out for yourself." He took a step toward the stairs, then turned back. "You don't tell him nothing," he said. "Nothing at all. If he lives through this, I don't want him to be able to find us."

She nodded, a chill settling in her. She was an outlaw now, too, and she'd made Archie one, as well. She'd shot a marshal and was holding him captive. She swallowed hard. "I'll let you know if he worsens."

Archie gave her a long, measured look. "You might want to put a drop or so of laudanum in the whiskey."

She stared at him in surprise. She knew they were running low.

"It will keep him quiet," Archie said. "That's what he needs, and what we need."

She nodded.

He gave her a sharp look. "We shouldn't have kept you here, girl."

She made a face. "You didn't keep me. My decision, remember."

"Mac should have insisted you go off to one of them fancy schools in Denver," he grumbled.

But Mac hadn't, not when she threatened to jump off the train and come back. She'd gotten all the schooling she needed from Reese and Mac.

"They would have tried to turn me into a lady."

He muttered something inaudible, then sighed heavily. "If he tries anything…"

She nodded. She was probably safer than Archie would be with the marshal. Archie had never been good with a gun. He could use a whip like it was part of his arm, but he'd never liked guns. He wasn't a fast draw or, with his fading sight, a good shot.

"And keep the door locked when you ain't there. Leave the key under the sack of coffee beans. We don't want anyone wandering into town and finding him."

"Not likely," she replied.

"*He* found his way here," Archie retorted. "Might be others comin' behind him."

Sam watched him as he moved slowly up the stairs. She found a tin cup and followed him up. He poured several drops of laudanum into it, then she left, hurrying down to the kitchen. She added a little whiskey to disguise the laudanum, then filled the cup with water from the pump.

The marshal was still unconscious, or seemed to be. She used some water in the pitcher to dampen a cloth, then sat in the chair and wiped the sweat from his face.

He groaned. His eyes flickered, then opened, and he stared at Sam. A muscle moved at the edge of his throat.

She studied him for a long moment, noting again the dark, taut skin stretched over high cheekbones, the thick eyebrows framing midnight-blue eyes.

A hard face with hard eyes. A face that looked as if he didn't smile much. Or laugh. A sudden empathy filled her, and she had the most ridiculous need to see him smile.

Remember Mac. Remember why this man came here.

Their gazes caught, and again she felt something new and powerful spark a response in her body.

She felt rooted to the floor, though her legs were trembling.

He tried to move, and a muscle tightened in his neck as he fell back. "I was trying to get some water...."

"You were on the floor," she said. "You must have fallen."

"Did you get me up...by yourself?"

"Archie and me."

"Where is he?"

She tried to fight off the intimacy that unexpectedly heated the room. "He had better things to do than nursemaid you."

He didn't reply, but suddenly his body tensed. She knew pain had struck again.

She offered him a drink from the tin cup. "I put a little whiskey in it," she said. He took it in his two hands, but they were unsteady and he spilled some despite what seemed to be an intense concentration. She leaned over and steadied his grip. He drank the cup dry.

She felt his forehead. Hot. He was too hot.

"Trying to get up was a damn fool thing to do," she said.

"Not as foolish...as shooting a marshal," he shot back.

"Brave words in your position," she replied. "I can always finish what I started."

He tried to move again and succeeded this time, but only a

few inches. He sank back against the pillow and closed his eyes as if he was too tired to keep them open. The attempt to stand had taken everything left in him.

His breathing was ragged, then calmed. The whiskey was getting to him, or maybe that drop of laudanum.

She pulled up a chair and sat down. She would wait until she was sure he was asleep. Then she had much to do. They had to be ready to leave as soon as Mac could travel.

But all she could focus on was the figure in the bed, the face tight with pain even in the drugged sleep. She wondered whether those midnight eyes would haunt her forever.

5

TWO DAYS WENT BY in a blur.

On the third day, Sam woke and looked out the window to see pouring rain. At least it should lower the abnormally high temperatures that had tormented both injured men.

She stretched. She'd spent all her time lately caring for the marshal and making preparations to leave Gideon's Hope as soon as Mac was well enough to ride. That meant cutting what meat they had into long strips and smoking it. She also used much of their remaining flour to make hardtack, a laborious process that produced a tasteless cracker. But hardtack didn't spoil and lasted forever. It was perfect for a long journey where fuel for the body was more important than taste.

She also started a stew from a venison roast, using carrots and potatoes and a number of herbs.

But uppermost in her mind were the two injured men. Archie stayed with Mac and, except for brief inspections and help with the chamber pot, he left the marshal's care up to her. The marshal was still weak from loss of blood and still in a great deal of pain. The laudanum she'd been slipping him helped him sleep, but he had a fever that worried her. Several times, she'd heard him call for someone named Sarah. She wondered if that was the name he'd called that first night. She couldn't help but wonder who Sarah was.

Wife? Lover?

He wore no ring, but that didn't mean anything. Still, there was no tintype of a woman in his saddle bags. No miniature. If she meant that much to him, wouldn't there be something?

The idea plagued her, and it shouldn't. She shouldn't care whether the marshal loved someone. It shouldn't matter at all.

And yet in the past couple days of caring for him, the connection she'd felt had grown stronger. She tried to tell herself it was only her usual feelings for a hurt critter. Empathy. That was all. But she was intrigued with the marshal's quiet stoicism mixed with a rare glimpse of wry humor and self-deprecation. She found herself longing to see a real smile.

Unlikely under the circumstances.

He showed signs of improvement this morning. The redness around the wound was fading.

She dressed quickly and ran a brush through her tousled curls. She checked on Mac first. He was sleeping. So was Archie on a cot near him. Quietly closing the door, she went downstairs. She started a fire in the stove. Archie would want his coffee soon. So would she.

She unlocked the door to the marshal's room. To her surprise he was awake, half sitting up in bed. She'd provided him with the shirt she'd found in his saddlebags, but it was unbuttoned and his chest was highly visible. The sun creases around his eyes were a little deeper. The dark bristles on his cheek made him look even more dangerous. The sheet was gathered around his waist.

He looked better, though. The last remnants of the laudanum were obviously gone. His eyes were sharp and penetrating. The pain was still strong. She could tell by the muscle working in his cheek. And his face was slightly flushed.

She wanted to touch his cheek to see how warm it was, but she knew now that to do so would unleash those wayward reactions inside her and, no doubt, bring a flush to her own cheeks. She couldn't give him that knowledge. That control.

"I'll have some coffee and breakfast soon," she said. "How does your leg feel?"

He raised an eyebrow. "Like it has a bullet hole in it."

If he meant to make her feel guilty, he succeeded. His gaze moved over her slowly, as if he were examining every part of her, inside and out. But he gave no indication of approval or disapproval, just watchfulness. She wondered what he saw. Anything more than an outlaw who'd shot him? She was suddenly aware of the loose shirt and worn pants she wore. She was definitely wanting in womanly refinement.

Her legs felt rubbery, and her heart beat faster. "You look better."

"Do I now?"

"Yes. Much. I think you might live after all."

"And that presents a problem, doesn't it?" He gave her a twisted smile, one that held a dare and even a hint of mockery.

He was obviously strong enough to confront what they'd both ignored these past several days. "Yes," she replied.

He looked disconcerted by her answer. "What have you been giving me?" he asked.

"A little laudanum," she replied. "To help you rest after that fall."

His expression told her he didn't believe that was the entire reason. "Why are you risking so much to protect a killer?"

She studied him. "How many men have *you* killed?"

He didn't reply, but a weariness appeared in his eyes. It almost made him seem vulnerable, took some of the hardness from his face and softened something in her.

She didn't want to acknowledge that. Not that or the raw longing deep inside her. "You kill for a living," she said more sharply than she intended. "Nothing to brag about in my eyes."

"Yet you protect…a woman-killer."

"A woman? Not Mac. You're after the wrong man."

"Ask him."

She shrugged. She couldn't let him know Mac was just above him. "I don't have to. Anyway, he isn't here."

"Then…why try to kill me…if he's not here?"

"If I'd really tried, you would be dead." She ignored the last part of the question.

His eyes burned into her. They were bright. Maybe too bright. "If you...weren't a woman, *you* would be dead. It may not work next time...." His voice trailed off.

Sam didn't believe him. Didn't want to believe that he thought her too weak to fight on his terms. "Keep thinking that," she retorted. "I can take care of myself."

"Maybe," he said. "But there are others coming, and you and an old man won't have a chance."

A lie. It had to be a lie to scare her. He would not have come alone if it were true.

Electricity crackled, the heated energy that often flashed between them when they sparred.

Sam forced herself to move. To break that connection. She poured him a cup of the lukewarm water left in the pitcher and started to hand it to him. His hand shook.

"You'll have to help me again," he said. "I might spill it." His gaze held hers—locked with hers—and it was far more of a challenge than an admission of weakness. She hesitated. Every time she neared him, something went amok inside her. Still, she sat on the edge of the bed. She put an arm around his neck and raised his head high enough to drink. She guided the cup to his mouth and he took several sips. Her other hand warmed where it touched his skin and his dark hair tickled her fingers. She felt a tightness in her chest and a flooding confusion.

"You his woman?" he asked quietly.

She was so lost in her own reactions, it took her several seconds to understand what he meant.

"Mac?" she blurted out in surprise. She pulled her hand away. Slowly. Reluctant to relinquish his touch.

"I didn't mean...Smith," he said with a twist of his lips. Speculation filled his dark eyes.

She started to tell him he was wrong, then stopped. Let him think what he wanted. He probably wouldn't believe her anyway.

He looked at her fingers. "No ring," he noted. "How does it happen that a pretty girl like you is unmarried?"

The change of subject was abrupt, and his voice was deeper.

Huskier. Almost seductive. Her breathing slowed and she felt a tightness in her throat.

Pretty. Mac and Reese had called her pretty, but she'd always discounted it. They were prejudiced.

And this man wanted something, she warned herself. He wanted to be free to take Mac. Still, she felt a rush of…pleasure at the compliment. She felt something else, too, a trembling along the length of her spine.

Run, she told herself. Run.

"Sam?" he asked, his dark eyebrows arching. "Is that your real name? Or is it Samantha?"

Her given name sounded fine on his tongue. As if he was tasting something delectable. The sudden change in tone—from harsh to tantalizing—was startling.

"It's Sam," she insisted. Sam was safer than Samantha at the moment.

"Then thank you, Sam."

"What for?" she asked suspiciously.

"The water, the whiskey…the nursing."

"Even if I shot you?"

"I'm *not* thanking you for that," he said, the side of his mouth quirking up in that intriguing half smile. "But you could have left me there."

She swallowed hard. He was being reasonable, yet she didn't believe a word of it. "I have chores to do," she said, but didn't take a step.

His hand rested on hers. Electricity passed between them again, raw and vital. She was excruciatingly aware of it.

"Why?" he persisted. "Why are you…living in this godforsaken place? You should be going to dances and having children and…"

"It's not godforsaken to me. It's beautiful, and I'm doing exactly what I want."

"Shooting strangers down in the street?" His voice was curiously empty of anger despite the harsh words. Guilt filled her again. She suspected he knew exactly what he was doing.

"Or did the man you call Mac put you up to it?" he continued in a conversational tone. "Does he always use a woman to fight his battles?"

He was baiting her now, challenging her with those dark eyes, with the sensuous twist of his lips. A sexually charged challenge that she couldn't step back from.

"He couldn't put me up to anything," she lied. "He isn't here."

"Do you know he killed two men just days ago?"

"You're sure of that?"

Those dark eyes met her gaze. "I'm sure. And there's more warrants."

She shrugged. "He's blamed for a lot of things he didn't do."

His hand traced a pattern on hers. "Such loyalty." He said it in a mocking tone but for a second she saw something else flicker in his gaze. A dark shadow that until now had been hidden behind those inscrutable eyes. She'd suspected that he was a man who was alone. A man who believed in little other than himself. But now she saw something else. An emptiness that made her melt inside.

She wanted to touch him. She wanted to wipe away the furrow between his brows, and ease the lines of pain that framed his face. She was mortified to realize there were tears welling behind her eyes.

Go. She started to stand, but his hand stopped her.

"Don't leave," he said. It was a plea more than a demand, and the need in the words stilled her.

It was hard to associate need with this man, and yet he was alone, in pain, in a hot, stuffy room with little to do but wonder what was going to happen to him.

A muscle moved slightly in his cheek and she had the impression of emotions under tight control again. "Another drink, perhaps?" he added.

Her hand shook slightly as she poured more water in his glass. But as she reached out to give it to him, his fingers met hers and he pulled her down. The cup slipped from her, splashing the contents down his chest. She started to jerk away but his fingers tightened around hers. Even as wounded as he was, there was an alertness in his eyes, a danger radiating from him that both frightened and excited her. Any remnant of vulnerability was gone. Or had she only imagined it?

Her body pressed against his, his warmth radiating through her, his heart pounding under hers. Heat spiked through her. She felt once again as if she'd just been hit by lightning.

In a brief flurry of panic, she tried to lean back. As his hand pressed her closer, she trembled from the waves of sensation that swept over her.

His lips were light against hers, barely touching. More like a feather drawn across her mouth. It was intoxicating, more than intoxicating. She wanted more.

Her body quivered ever so slightly as his lips invited her mouth to open. He deepened the kiss, moving his mouth against hers with a fierce urgency. And then she was drowning in new sensations.

His arm, stronger than she'd believed possible after the loss of blood, kept her bound to him. She knew she could force herself free by hitting his wounded leg, but part of her didn't want to move. As if he knew everything she felt, his mouth pressed hard against hers. For the first time she started to understand the need between a man and a woman, the feelings that drove them to be together. He opened his mouth and she felt the invasion of his tongue, and she welcomed it, marveling at how it could awaken so many senses in her....

He was her enemy. Mac's enemy.

The thought pierced the web of sensation. Horrified at herself, she struggled against his arm.

To her surprise, he let go and fell back on the bed, breathing hard. His eyes closed for a moment, and when they opened again they were flat. The muscles in his chest were taut with strain, and his breath came in labored spurts.

He must have jarred his wounded leg. Or the effort of holding her had sapped what strength he had.

She scrambled away before he could reach out for her

again. She still felt the heat from his chest, the touch of his warm skin.

She tried not to look as flustered and confused as she felt. She was sure he could hear her heart beating. "I'll...I'll be back later with a poultice for that wound. You didn't help it when..." She was at a loss to continue to describe what had just happened.

He looked as stunned as she was, but managed an expression that was half grimace, half surprise. "It...was worth it," he said.

She escaped before she blurted out something silly.

Once outside, she leaned against the wall and took long deep breaths. *What had just happened?*

The books she'd read hadn't lied after all.

As THE DOOR CLOSED, Jared lay back on the hard bed and fought the pain. The wound hurt like the furies in hell, but he'd survived worse and had been on his feet within hours. He had the constitution of a horse, according to a friend, and he'd prepared himself for the pain.

He hadn't been prepared, though, when another part of his body started aching, as well. He hadn't expected the firestorm that suddenly erupted between Sam and him.

He'd kissed her in an effort to discover more about her. At least that's what he told himself. And now he was left aching, and she was more of a mystery than ever.

Jared was usually good at judging people, but he couldn't figure her out. She was a bundle of contradictions. Tough enough to shoot a lawman face-on. Then minutes later healing with gentle hands.

He had thought she must be Thornton's wife or mistress. He'd taken her into his arms under that assumption. He'd felt no guilt in doing so.

The kiss had proved him wrong. The surprise on her face gave her away. So did the confusion when he'd first pressed his lips to hers, the awakening in her eyes as she'd instinctively responded to them...and then pulled back in a kind of wonderment.

He would bet his next month's salary she was a virgin. An innocent.

None of this made sense. Not the woman. Not this sorry excuse for a town. Not the old man. And surely not the outlaw who now called himself MacDonald. Sam and the old man had talked about him like he was some kind of God.

Sam. Hell of a name for a woman. And she *was* a woman. Despite the physical awkwardness of their positions on the bed, he'd felt her softness through the clothes, and her short hair had been like silk. And smelled of roses.

A paradox. A woman equally gifted in inflicting pain and easing it.

He closed his eyes. He was still weak from the loss of blood. Maybe that was why he damn well couldn't think beyond the woman. She intrigued him far more than she should. Still, maybe he could use that unexpected attraction. Damn, he'd been angry and in more than a little pain, and yet he'd felt a growing need inside. Didn't make any sense.

And he would bet his life that she felt something, too. She'd run like a startled doe.

Whatever relationship she had with Thornton, Jared had no compunction about using her. Despite what his fellow marshals claimed about his dour disposition, he could be charming enough when necessary. He was rusty as hell, but he was running out of options.

He managed to move up in the bed but at a cost. *Strength.* He had to get his strength back.

He wanted to put his legs down, test them, but he didn't want to end up on the floor again. Patience, he warned himself. But he didn't have much time. Thornton couldn't be far away.

His fingers tightened into a fist at the thought. So close to his quarry, so close to justice for Emma. *Because she had trusted him.*

Just as his wife had.

Jared closed his eyes. Usually when he did that, his last thought before sleep was of Sarah. Now it was a tall spitfire with dagger eyes and a quick tongue. Sam with the short, light brown hair and golden eyes.

Sarah had had long hair the color of wheat. He'd loved that hair, particularly at night when she brushed it before twisting it into one long braid.

Sarah...who'd been small and gentle, everything he'd ever thought he wanted in a wife. She had never wanted anything more than Jared and children.

Pain ripped through him. Not physical this time, but the kind that came with memories. He remembered the last time he saw her. The war had started, and he felt strongly he should go. His brother and his wife lived nearby and would look after the farm and Sarah. Jared was the marksman, the hunter. His brother, Seth, was the farmer.

He hadn't known Sarah was with child, nor had he thought the war would last as long as it did. A few months, he'd figured. No more. Instead he was sent to Texas, then Mississippi and finally Virginia. He learned he had a daughter when a letter finally reached him, and he'd dreamed about holding her. He counted off her birthdays.

After the war ended, he headed home, all his restlessness tamed. He was going home!

All he'd found were graves.

Only Emma, his sister-in-law, had been spared. She was teaching at the school.

Spared only to die in a stagecoach robbery.

By the man Sam was determined to protect.

HER HEART STILL POUNDING hard, Sam ran up the stairs to her room. She splashed water from a pitcher on her face, willing the flush to fade from her cheeks. Then she changed from her drenched shirt to a clean one.

Nearly every fiber of her being was sizzling. The books *were* right. She *had* trembled. The temperature in the room did rise. Her world did turn upside down. Her skin had burned from his touch, and her lips continued to feel the magical impact of his kiss.

She tried not to think of those few moments, or her monumental lapse in judgment. Something the lawman said nagged at her. He'd told her that someone else might be after Mac, as well.

With shaky fingers she ran a brush through her hair, then left the room and took the few steps to Mac's. She stood outside the hall for a moment. Her legs were weak from the kiss, and her heart was beating a little too rapidly.

Willing herself to relax, she knocked on the door before opening it.

Archie, snoring loudly, sat in a chair beside Mac. Mac was not moving. His face was bright with fever, and he was covered with blankets despite the heavy smell of sweat in the room.

His gun hand was swathed with bandages, and he looked years older than he had in the days before his trip. He'd always been bigger than life to her. He'd been her protector for most of her life, and now *he* needed protection. It was the only gift she could give him.

Archie woke with a jerk but came immediately alert. "Somethin' wrong, Sam?"

"I don't know. Maybe the marshal's lying, but there might be a problem."

He waited for her to go on.

"He says there's others coming after Mac."

"He didn't say anything more?"

"No." She could hardly admit she had basically fled the room shortly after. "I thought he was just trying to scare me."

He gave her a long look. "Could be," he said. "Wouldn't hurt to ask Jake and Ike to watch the pass. You can talk to them in the morning. Won't be anyone coming down that way tonight."

Sam nodded.

"The marshal must be doing all right if he's talkin' so much."

"He's still in pain, but he's not one to give in to it."

"You might ask him who he thinks is coming," Archie said.

"And you watch him real close. I wish I could take over for you, but…"

"I'll be fine. You just take care of Mac." She hesitated. "He isn't any better, is he?"

"I have to git that fever down. Then…mebbe he'll have a chance. I want you to make some more poultices for him. Make one for the marshal, too."

She nodded. She'd planned to do that today. "I just thought you should know what the marshal said."

He hesitated. "You did right."

She left, feeling better that Archie knew. They couldn't take chances. Not with Mac so badly injured.

At least Archie was here with her. A mule skinner, he'd joined the army during the Mexican American war and was assigned to take care of the hospital wagons and horses. When they weren't traveling, he helped the few doctors. They found him a willing pupil. Then he expanded his knowledge by living with the Utes for several years and learning their herbal medicines. Sam couldn't help but smile at the tales he told, many times over, of his brushes with death. She'd never known what was true and what wasn't. What she did know was that he was very skilled at healing people, better, many said, than a trained physician.

Sam made the poultices, a mixture of turpentine, herbs and moss heated together and placed on a section of sheet. She then warmed some whiskey and crushed willow bark. She took the poultice and a cup of the whiskey up to Archie for Mac. Then she steeled herself before returning to the marshal's room.

She would not be affected by him this time. She wouldn't go nearer than absolutely necessary. She wouldn't engage him in personal conversation.

She *would* ask him to explain his comment about others coming for Mac.

Loaded down with her tray of supplies and a lantern, she stepped into the room. The marshal was on his side. He turned toward her and leaned on an elbow. "I thought you ran away," he said gruffly.

"I never run away," she said indignantly. "I had to make a poultice for the wound." She pushed the pillow behind his head until they were high enough for him to drink easily.

He glanced at the cup in her hand suspiciously. "What is it?"

"Whiskey and willow bark. It will cut the pain when I put the poultice on."

He took the cup in two hands. Despite his drawn face, he looked lethal. He seemed to read every thought she had and keep secret all of his. She suspected he did that frequently. Fixed those dark eyes on some poor soul until they were thoroughly intimidated.

She wasn't going to be intimidated. Nor was she going to allow a repeat of what had happened earlier.

"I have a question," she said.

"And how can I help you, Miss Sam?"

"You said someone might be coming after Mac."

"Ah, you listened. I wasn't sure."

The man obviously wasn't going to offer anything else. "Who?" she asked.

He shrugged. "Name of Calhoun Benson. He claims your 'Mac' shot his son in cold blood. He's advertising for gunslingers. Fifty dollars each and a thousand for the man who kills MacDonald or Thornton or whatever name he goes by."

"Why are you telling me?"

"Oddly enough, I wouldn't want to see you or the old man in the line of fire. I would suggest you leave as soon as possible."

"And you?"

"I can manage."

"And then you'd go after this...man you're hunting?"

"Yes."

"Why?"

"I'm a marshal."

"But it's something more," she said. "I hear it in your voice when you mention him. Like it's personal."

He didn't answer, but his eyes turned icy as he drank from the cup.

Then, unexpectedly, his lips quirked up on one side. "I don't suppose you want to help me drink again."

"I think you're strong enough to hold that little cup," she replied.

He finished the whiskey, then handed the cup back to her. She tried to avoid his touch, but somehow...

His fingers covered hers, the heat from his hand scorching her skin and traveling like a brush fire through her bloodstream. For a moment, she thought he might try to grab her again, but his hand fell back. The half smile grew wider, and the dimple in his chin deepened. He looked...rakish.

Except there was no laughter or light in him. Even when he flashed that smile, she sensed it was all on the surface.

You shot him. Why should he have any joy or laughter?

She put the cup down, then removed the loose bandage around the wound. It was raw and seeping. She winced. Maybe she should wait until the morning.

"What's in the poultice?" he asked.

"Turpentine and moss and some of Archie's Indian herbs."

He nodded as if that was enough explanation.

"It's going to burn," she said, hesitating.

His gaze met hers. "I know the effect of turpentine. Go ahead."

"Do you need a piece of wood, something to bite on?"

"No," he said flatly.

She placed the poultice on the wound. His body tensed and his hands balled into fists. "Christ," he said.

She knew it had to be agonizing at first. The turpentine would draw out any poison, and then the moss and herbs would soothe, but that would take a while. Archie had used the same combination on her when she'd ripped her leg open after falling from her horse. "It'll keep the wound from putrefying," she tried to explain.

"If it doesn't kill me," he replied darkly.

"More whiskey?"

He nodded. She left the room, refilled the cup and returned. He drained it.

"Anything else I can do?" she asked.

"Another kiss, perhaps." His voice was slurred but his eyes were clear. And piercing.

A taunt? Or simply male reaction?

Ignore it. "I don't think so," she said, trying to keep her voice even. "Sleep well."

She grabbed the lantern and left, closing the door behind her and remembering to lock it this time. She was trembling. What frightened her more than anything was that she hadn't wanted to leave.

She wanted that kiss. Wanted it to the tip of her toes. She wondered whether it would be like the other one. Did kisses get better?

As hurting as he must be, he was still defiant. And dangerous. She suspected that he would not let her stand in the way of getting what he wanted. Even as she went up the stairs to get some sleep, she kept reliving that earlier kiss, the moment of magic when the world stopped turning for a fraction of an instant. Her body tingled with the remembrance of it, and she wished her mother was alive, that she had someone to talk to about it.

Was this the way her mother had felt when Mac kissed her? Had he turned her mother's life inside out? She tried to remember, but the two of them had been very careful around her. Very proper for the other boarders. But sometimes Sam caught them in an embrace. Had her mother felt this hunger inside? And where did it lead? The need to know more, to feel more, to experience more gnawed at her heart.

But the marshal didn't love her, and she certainly couldn't feel anything for him.

When she reached her room, she tried to ignore the ache deep within her, the sudden loneliness she'd never felt before.

She hadn't realized something was missing in her life. And there was nothing she could do about it.

6

AT FIRST LIGHT, Sam rode in a driving rain down to the stream about a half mile from town. Dawg ran alongside her horse, happy to be out for a run despite the rain.

Unfortunately, all Sam's thoughts were of the marshal.

She hadn't slept well. In fact she'd had little rest since his arrival. But she'd kept turning in bed. Wondering how it would feel to lie next to him. Wondering why her body was responding in such rebellious ways.

She'd checked on the marshal before leaving. He was sleeping, thank God. No dark eyes to probe straight to her core…

She stopped at one of the four cabins that had survived the fire and knocked on the door. A lanky old trapper in buckskins opened it. "Miss Sam, a pleasure for sure." He led the way inside, inviting Dawg, as well. "Now, what can I do for you?"

She quickly explained what had happened three days earlier, though she suspected Burley had already told Jake everything.

"Can you and Ike watch the pass?" she asked.

"Yeah, I'll take a turn at watching," Jake agreed. "So will Ike. He's out hunting now, but he should be back soon."

"Burley will relieve you, too," Sam said.

Jake snorted. "Can't depend on Burley."

"You can, if he says so," she replied. "He feels really bad that he admitted to the marshal that Mac might be in town."

Jake grumbled under his breath. "Damn fool." Then he turned his attention back to her.

"You really leaving Gideon's Hope?" he asked. "Archie said you plan to head north."

"When Mac's well enough. Maybe a week or so."

"We sure will miss you. You and Mac and Archie. Even Reese, damn his soul. No one left to win what little gold I pan."

"Come with us."

"No, Miss Sam. Been in these mountains too long. When I die, I want to be looking at them peaks. Like they're reaching up to heaven, they are. I can just follow them up."

She loved the mountains, too, and would miss them bitterly.

"You shoulda gone ahead and killed that marshal," Jake muttered. "Save you a lot of trouble. I ain't got no use for most of them."

Of course he didn't. Jake didn't like authority of any kind, which was why he and Archie got along so well. The mountain man had come to Gideon's Hope seven years ago with a load of furs and a body racked with pneumonia. Archie had treated him with some of his Indian remedies, and Jake gradually regained his strength. He'd returned the next four winters. When most of the population left, he'd appropriated one of the few remaining cabins. Getting too old, he said, to live up in the mountains alone year-round.

He was in his seventies now, a thin, wiry man but still strong enough to stay in the mountains by himself for months. If he said he would watch the pass, he would. Ike had been his friend for a long time, and he, too, had settled in an abandoned cabin next to the stream, mainly, she thought, to look after Jake. Neither one of them liked people much, and Gideon's Hope with its permanent population of seven suited both just fine. They hunted, fished and trapped. Archie was there if needed for healing, Mac to take a drink with and Reese to gamble with. No man needed more, he said.

It was a small ragtag group. Ike and Jake, Burley, Archie

and herself. If an army of gunslingers came for Mac, the five of them would have a hard time fighting them off. But they had an advantage. They knew every inch of the area. They could always hide Mac in one of the abandoned mines carved out of the rock. Not particularly healthy for him, but better than being hanged or shot.

"I'll go on up there now," Jake said. He looked down at his feet. "Maybe you can leave a note for Ike. Tell him to meet me there."

She gave him a quick hug and left. She'd offered to teach Jake to read and write, but he'd refused. Too old to learn new tricks, he always said. The rain had slackened slightly by the time she'd left a note in Ike's cabin and stopped to gather moss from around the trees along the creek. She would need it for the poultices; her supply was running low. Behind her were more mountains and an overgrown trail that led east through a narrow and steep pass. It was the only way into Gideon's Hope when the creek ran strong and deep as it did now. The pass was both their protection and their weak spot.

She stood a moment longer, drinking in the peace. She never grew tired of the view, especially in winter when the water glistened with ice and the trees with snow. But spring was grand, too, with its wildflowers and tender new shoots. Sometimes the landscape was so lovely it hurt.

She would miss it, but she also looked forward to a new adventure.

Sam went up to Mac's room. She knocked but opened the door before anyone answered.

Archie gave her a tired smile and nodded his head toward the bed. Mac's face was pale under its deep tan, but when she felt his cheek, it wasn't as hot as it was yesterday.

"His fever went down this morning," Archie said. "He's still damned weak, but I think he'll make it."

"He's conscious?"

"On and off. Mostly off. Still not making much sense. Muttering about your ma."

"I'll put some stew on. Just let me know when he wakes

again." She leaned over and touched Mac's good hand, taking it in hers, willing her strength into him.

"The marshal?" he asked.

"I put the poultice on the wound last night. I checked early this morning and he was asleep. His breathing was ragged, but he wasn't hot."

He nodded. "Strong as a damned mule. Damn if I know what we'll do with him."

She wondered the same thing. "I think he might be on his feet faster than we thought."

Archie muttered under his breath.

"I'll make some biscuits for breakfast."

"Naw, just some bread and that jam you made," he said. "And coffee."

"I'll have it here in a minute." She regarded Archie for a moment, then Mac, and her heart filled with love for both of them. They were all in danger. And the danger was downstairs in the form of a tall, taciturn man who set her whole being on fire.

She went over and gave Archie a rare hug. Clung to him, in fact. She couldn't talk to him about what was going on inside her, but she could absorb his affection, the acceptance of who and what she was.

"I don't know what I would do if I lost any one of you," she said before stepping back.

"One day…" he started to say, but she darted out the door before he could finish. She didn't want to hear about one day.

Her shirt was still damp, but she decided not to take the time to change it. Instead, she went directly to the kitchen and made coffee. She took one cup along with a plate of bread and jam up to Archie. Then she cut three more thick slices from the loaf and spread them with jam.

The marshal had been too weak to take anything but broth in the past few days, but she suspected that was changing.

She unlocked the door to his room and glanced inside. He was still sleeping. Or pretending to sleep. The sheet had fallen away from him.

She moved closer and put the food and coffee on the table. Then she studied him, particularly the scars she'd noticed yesterday. The war? How and when had he been hurt? His life obviously hadn't been easy.

The sheet was tangled, and he'd taken off the shirt again, probably because of the heat in the small, stuffy room. There was no way of getting pants over his wound and the poultice, and he was magnificent in his nakedness. She reached down and covered him as well as she could, forcing herself to concentrate on his face. His face only.

She longed to make him smile. Even laugh. *Don't lie.* She wanted more than that. She wanted him to touch her. Slowly. Seductively.

"Marshal?" She said the word softly. If he didn't wake, she didn't intend to rouse him. He needed rest.

He opened his eyes and rolled on his back. She didn't know whether he had been feigning sleep or whether her voice had awakened him.

He didn't reply. Instead he fixed her with that steady gaze of his. Waiting. He seemed to be a patient man. A man who waited for the right moment. A shiver ran through her.

"I've brought coffee and food."

He moved up in the bed to lean against the iron posts. A muscle worked along his throat as he made the effort.

"How's your leg?" she asked.

"Still hurts like hell."

Well, she'd asked. She decided to ignore the answer. "Want some coffee?"

He nodded even as he regarded her with an unblinking stare. There was calculation in his eyes, although the side of his lips had a quizzical turn to them. The dimple in his chin appeared to be deeper. He took the coffee and held it in both hands as he sipped.

The bristle on his face was darker, a little heavier, and he looked more bandit than lawman. For a split second, she saw a simmering anger behind his dark eyes before they went blank.

She remembered the image she'd had before of a wild animal waiting to pounce.

She prayed her face didn't give her wayward thoughts away. Instead she concentrated on the fact that he was a marshal. And not just any marshal. She took a deep breath and tried to understand why it was catching in her throat.

Sam suddenly remembered the bread on the table. She practically stumbled over herself to hand the plate to him. He put it in his lap and balanced the cup of coffee in one hand. He picked up a slice of bread and bit off a large chunk, leaving jam smeared over his lips. For a moment, he looked like a lad, and she grinned at the incongruous sight.

He seemed perplexed for a moment, then he used his tongue to wipe his lips clean. Slowly. Seductively. Her pulse quickened and her legs felt boneless.

"I didn't realize how hungry I was," he said, taking another bite as something like satisfaction spread over his face, giving it life for the first time.

Something shifted inside of her as an almost palpable attraction leaped between them, filling the air with its intensity. Maybe Reese had been right. Maybe she *had* been here too long. Maybe she would have felt the same no matter who rode into their town.

But she really didn't think so.

She glanced down and immediately wished he still wore the shirt. His shoulders were wide and his chest was corded with muscle.

Strength and power. And will. They were in his face, evident in the lack of emotion he showed. Drat him. How could he be so controlled when her stomach was churning and her heart rocked back and forth? She looked up to meet his eyes again. Nothing in them but a cool, calculating perusal, and yet she sensed danger, the way one senses the approach of a death-dealing storm.

When he finished, she took the empty plate from him. It was warm from his hands. "I'll…I'll be making some stew later," she said.

"I'll be waiting," he replied. Invitation was in his voice, but she wasn't exactly sure what kind of invitation it was. Maybe a cat's to a mouse.

She tried to ignore it, tried to avoid his eyes, which seemed to focus on the still-damp shirt that clung to her. She removed the poultice from his leg and studied the wound. It was still seeping, but she saw no sign of infection. She was only too aware that he wasn't looking at it; instead his eyes were fixed on her face.

"Looks like it's beginning to heal." Sam tried to make the words matter-of-fact, but she feared there was a breathless quality to them. "I'll bring a fresh poultice later."

"You like torturing people, then?" he said with a twist of his lips that belied the words.

"You can die, instead," she offered amicably.

He mulled that over for a moment. "Not much of a choice." He shrugged. "You can have your way with me."

An innuendo. She decided to ignore it.

"Where's the old man—Smith?" he asked suddenly.

The question took her by surprise. "Busy," she said after a few long seconds.

"He was...so protective," he observed. "I wonder why he's leaving you alone with me."

His voice was stronger than yesterday, although she knew from the muscle in his throat that every movement was an effort.

"I don't think you're going anywhere for a while," she said. "Unless, of course, you want to damage that leg permanently. Maybe lose it."

Speculation was still evident in his gaze. "I have to admit you're easier on the eyes than Smith."

She didn't know how to reply to that.

"You didn't say *where* he is," the marshal persisted.

"He has better things to do than treat a marshal," she replied, trying to keep her voice steady, not let him know how much he affected her. "And he trusts me. I've been assisting him for years."

"So many talents," he said. "I'm impressed. You can shoot. You can nurse. You can cook. You're even a prison guard. What more do you do?" The tone was light, even bantering, but she didn't miss the dangerous glint in his eyes.

"More than you'll ever know about," she retorted as the air grew denser between them.

"Maybe," he said. Then, as he'd done before, he abruptly changed the subject. She wondered whether he'd felt the heightened temperature as she did. "Where's that huge beast of yours?"

"Dawg?"

"Do you have another one?"

"Not at the moment."

"What else do you do in this town besides look after an old man and the assorted marshals who wander in?"

"A lot of things, and you ask way too many questions."

"I'm a curious man." He smiled then. It was a crooked smile, but she detected a real one behind it this time.

"Sam?" he said. "It's taking me some time to get used to that name. You're much too…pretty for it."

The *pretty* word again.

She suspected he meant to throw her off balance, to discover something he wanted to know. Yet he said her name as though he was tasting the sound of it on his tongue, letting it linger in the air. "Sam what?"

She remembered what Jake had told her about not revealing any information. "Just Sam," she said.

"Tell me more about Thornton."

She shrugged. "He helped raise me. He protected me. And if there's anything I can tell you, it's that he would never, never hurt a woman."

He raised an eyebrow. "Nothing else?"

She felt blood rising to her face. That he thought…

"He's family. And a friend. If you know what that means?"

"A friend doesn't use a friend to do his dirty work." He

was pushing for information again and not being very subtle about it.

"No," she replied agreeably.

She saw the frustration in his face. She even enjoyed it a little, considering how *he* had rattled her last night.

"I heard that one of those two men he killed wounded him," he said.

His words sent a chill through her. "Wouldn't know anything about that."

"Why is his horse here, then?"

"If you believe anything old Burley says, then that leg isn't the only thing that has a hole in it. Mac has several horses. He traded me that paint last time he passed through. He took a bay. It was faster."

"What happened to your parents?" he asked, his voice suddenly softening.

"My pa was killed by a claim jumper when I was real young. My mother had no family, no place to go, so she stayed here. She cooked meals for the miners and did their laundry. She eventually opened a boardinghouse but died of pneumonia when I was eleven."

"No other family?"

She shrugged. "Both of them were orphans."

The marshal waited for her to continue.

She wasn't sure she wanted to, and yet she needed him to know that Mac wasn't the man he thought him to be. "After my mother died, the miners held a meeting and were going to send me to an orphanage. Mac and Archie wouldn't let them do it. They sort of adopted me." She purposely left Reese's name out.

"So Thornton helped raise you," he said, returning to the earlier subject.

"Some," she said, unwilling to give him any more information.

He lifted a thick eyebrow. "He kept you here in the middle of nowhere. You…should be…" He moved slightly, then stiffened and she knew a wave of pain had just hit. He closed his eyes for a second. "Damn," he muttered.

She waited, not saying anything. She wanted to do something to soothe the pain. She forced herself not to go closer.

Then his body started to relax slowly.

"I'm here because I want to be here," she said softly.

"A ghost town these last five years? What about school?"

"Reese…" she started, then caught herself. "I learned from books," she said.

"Reese?" The question was sharp, his eyes relentless despite the pain in his face.

She snapped her mouth shut. Would Reese be held accountable for being Mac's friend? Or even for being her friend? She was an outlaw now, too. She'd shot a marshal.

Leave, she told herself. *Leave now.* But something kept her feet planted firmly where she was.

"How long since your family came here?" he asked again, obviously intent on finding out whatever he could. Looking for a weakness, she supposed.

He would find none in her, but there was no harm in this question. "Pa came here in 1858," she said.

Dear God, but his eyes were compelling. She knew what he was doing. Information was a weapon.

"When did Thornton arrive?" he asked.

Thornton. Not Mac. Cal Thornton. That was how she first knew him. When he stayed in her mother's boardinghouse. She'd already said too much. The marshal was good at extracting information. Very good. She'd never known exactly how Mac had got his reputation, or why he'd been wanted. They didn't talk about that. She did know, though, that his past was the reason he'd never married her mother. She also knew he'd been a hired gun on and off. But she would never believe he'd killed a woman as the marshal claimed.

She didn't answer. Instead, she defended Mac. "You're wrong about him," she said flatly.

"Then he should go back with me. Prove the accusations false."

"You said he killed a woman. When?"

"Ten years ago."

"How?"

"He was robbing a stagecoach."

"Anyone see him kill her?"

"The guy who rode with him. Before he hanged. And the coach driver heard his name."

"Ever consider he might have a reason for lying?"

"Doesn't matter. Thornton rode with him. He's just as guilty. And guilty of a hell of a lot more, as well."

"You a judge as well as a lawman?"

His eyes grew even colder, if that was possible. "You aren't doing yourself or anyone here a favor by hiding him."

"Threats don't scare me. They just make it more likely Mac will kill you."

"Your...Mr. Smith said Mac wouldn't like you killing me."

"Me. He wouldn't like *me* killing someone. Doesn't mean he wouldn't do it himself. He's a 'killer,' remember." Anger raised her voice, and she saw satisfaction deep in his eyes. He'd scored a small victory. He was pulling little nuggets of information from her, and she was allowing it. Turnabout was fair play.

"And you? Have you always been a marshal?"

"No," he said.

"Then what?"

"A farmer," he said softly.

"What turned a farmer into a marshal?"

"The war," he said shortly.

"Reb or Yank?"

He searched her face again. "Does it matter?"

"Not really. That's one reason my father and mother left Illinois. They wanted no part of it. All those men killed...homes destroyed... Mac's home was one of them."

His face tightened and his eyes were like black agates. That strange feeling kicked her stomach again. His gaze speared her as if he could see the very essence of her soul. "Mine was, too. I didn't turn outlaw."

His tone sent shivers through her. Harsh. Unforgiving. Relentless. There was no gentleness in him. None of the wry humor she'd glimpsed a few times.

"Maybe not, but it seems to me you're as much a killer as you say Mac is." She glared at him. "Are you always so certain you're right?"

To her surprise, he shook his head. Then he added, with the slightest hint of a smile, "But more often than not."

"I doubt that," she muttered.

He ignored the comment and held out his cup. "Any water left?"

The pitcher was still on the table and she poured water for him. It turned brown from the remnants of coffee.

He took it and drank deeply.

She couldn't keep her eyes from his face. From the lips that had covered hers yesterday. She could still feel them, and the reactions they had stirred in her. Damn him, why did he have to be even more appealing with the dark stubble on his cheeks. Maybe it was his confidence, even as a prisoner. He was a man used to being heeded and obeyed.

Go. Go. Go. Go.

But her legs didn't move.

"Sam?"

Her name had never quite sounded like that before. The one syllable rolled lazily on his lips.

"Yes?" she forced herself to reply.

"I meant it when I warned you to leave. I wouldn't like to see you hurt. If what you say about Thornton is true, he wouldn't want it, either."

She heard the doubt in his voice about Mac, and it spoiled any concern she thought he might have for her.

She walked to the door. "I'll be back later with some stew and a fresh poultice for your leg."

"It's comforting to know you're so interested in my well-being," he said in a soft, dangerous tone.

"I'm not," she replied. "I just don't want you to die here."

"Why? There's plenty of places to bury a body."

"I'm thinking about all of them at this moment," she said.

He closed his eyes, but the left side of his mouth drifted up.

Damn the man. She didn't understand why she was drawn to him. Or why she wanted to touch that hard face and make it soften.

"A little gratitude would be nice," she said, knowing it was a mistake to linger. "Archie did save your leg."

"He wouldn't have needed to, if you hadn't shot me," he replied.

There was some justification in his words, she admitted to herself. But then he shouldn't have come after Mac.

"Why are you so determined?" she asked. "It's not just because Mac's wanted. You've been looking for him for years." It wasn't exactly a stab in the dark. She'd detected something in his tone when he spoke Mac's name. By the sudden chill in his eyes, she knew she was right.

He stared at her, and she wished she saw something in his eyes. The nothingness was frightening. Far more frightening than the anger or contempt. There was a very personal motivation behind his hunt, and it was deep and strong. She knew then that he would never give up.

She shook off the chill that ran through her and opened the door.

"Samantha?" His words stopped her and she turned around.

"Sam will do."

"I like Samantha better." His eyes suddenly seemed to undress her with a lazy sensuality, removing her clothes piece by piece.

Painfully exquisite sensations started to boil in her core. Sparks shot between them, live and biting. Intense. She knew she was losing control, floundering in depths she didn't understand.

She saw surprise in his eyes, as if he, too, felt something he didn't want to feel.

"You'd better go, Miss Samantha," he said. His words were mocking, as if he knew exactly what was going on inside her.

She swallowed hard and followed his advice. A little too quickly.

Damn him.

She went into the small kitchen off the bar. She was shaking, buffeted by conflicting emotions. She feared him for Mac's sake, but something in her was reacting to him in a way she'd never reacted to a man before. She was drawn to him as if she were a piece of metal and he a magnet.

She stirred the pot of venison stew hanging in the fireplace and added some water. She'd started it yesterday while the marshal slept and continually added water and spices, siphoning the broth for Mac.

Then she found the key to the marshal's room and turned it in the lock. No ordinary man would be walking for another week, but she knew now he was not like other men.

He was an enemy. A danger to those she loved.

She shouldn't care anything about him.

And, hell's blazes, she didn't.

7

JARED WATCHED her go, heard the key turn in the lock a few minutes later.

He wanted to throw something, but there was nothing but the cup and a tin pitcher of water, and then he would be without. Dammit, she hadn't listened to him.

No doubt she thought he was lying. He wished to hell he was.

Maybe he could talk some sense into the old man.

Or maybe Thornton—MacDonald—was the reason she wouldn't leave. Maybe he was nearby or due to be here soon. And where was the man called Reese? A woman and two old men—Archie and the stableman—alone, for God's sake.

He didn't want her hurt. Despite the fact she'd shot him, he couldn't avoid seeing the war being waged inside her. He was sure now that she hadn't tried to kill him. She was too intent on saving him. She'd taken a hell of a chance in confronting him under those circumstances, and she'd tried to do what she could to fix his leg and alleviate his pain.

She'd held a gun and shot well enough to have been taught by an expert. He had no doubt that the expert was Thornton. The outlaw must have told her that if she aimed a gun at someone, she had to be willing to kill. *Thornton*. She must care for him a great deal to do what she'd done—it so obviously went against everything she seemed to be.

That notion ripped through his soul. Although she did her best not to show it, there was a gentleness—even tenderness—in her that made what she'd done a powerful testament to the bond between her and Thornton.

He'd thought in the beginning she must be Thornton's woman. Now he knew the outlaw had been a father-figure.

It all fit. There was an innocence in her that touched something he thought firmly dead. She'd been completely unaware of how damn desirable she'd looked when she entered his room, a damp shirt and trousers pasted to her body and her hair swirling about her face in tiny ringlets. Another part of him had started to ache then. It made the pain of his wound minor in comparison.

And when he'd kissed her last night...there had been no mistaking the shock in her eyes, and she'd responded so briefly with a mixture of instinctive need and curiosity that touched and fascinated him.

This attraction was obviously new to her. And to him. For a moment last night he'd forgotten who and what she was. It had been a long time since he'd felt something more than a simple physical need for a woman. He'd seen too much tragedy and death not to barricade his heart. He hadn't wanted to feel. Now was not the time to let someone tear down those barriers.

But he *had* felt something. Then and now. She was such an intriguing combination of woman and girl. He discovered a new facet every time he saw her. She was smart and quick and competent in so many ways, and yet there was a beguiling naturalness about her.

Now he knew at least part of her story. Losing a father, then a mother while still a child. Left orphaned in a lawless mining town with an outlaw as protector. Loving one, it seemed. He took a deep breath as the implication sank in. Nothing he'd learned so far fit the man he'd hunted all these years.

Maybe he *was* wrong. Maybe this Mac wasn't Thornton after all.

None of it made sense to him. And he didn't like things that didn't make sense.

He pictured her again as she'd left the room. How had he ever, even for a second, mistaken her for a boy? She was all feminine grace, and completely unaware of it. Those eyes took a man's breath away when they focused on him. Even when she tried to conceal something, they gave her away. Except for that moment in the street, the moment when she had put everything she was into convincing him she meant to kill him. And that said something about her, too.

He smiled inwardly at her headlong flight last night. He would wager she didn't have much experience with men. And that meant Thornton wasn't quite the rogue Jared had thought him to be. Maybe the man *had* done something decent, but that didn't negate the fact he was a murderer.

As for himself...

He had to tamp down his attraction to her. Since his wife had died, he'd known women, but they had always been experienced, and none of them expected more than a few hours of physical pleasure. He'd never wanted to feel what he felt that day he'd returned from the war. He'd never wanted to feel that kind of pain again.

He hadn't imagined ever letting go of even a small piece of himself again, and yet Sam's vulnerability threatened to snatch something no other woman had been able to touch.

He changed positions, inviting pain. He needed reminders as to why the pain was there. He'd searched too long for Thornton, and the woman was his key to finding him. It was not only his job, but a debt he owed his wife and sister-in-law.

He wasn't going to let anyone stand in his way. Not even a bewitching little temptress named Sam.

SAM TRIED not to think of the marshal as she went about her morning chores.

Everything had been so different just a short while ago. They'd been getting ready to leave. She'd been canning vegetables and smoking meat and fish for their journey. She'd resigned herself to leaving the valley and was even feeling a bit of anticipation. Then Mac rode in, more dead than alive.

And until Jared came four days ago, she hadn't known she could tingle down to her toes when she was with a man. That her heart could beat so fast and her blood run hot. The marshal had awakened feelings and sensations she hadn't known existed, a craving for some unknown yet irresistible wonder, an awareness of her own vulnerability.

She finished washing the cloths they'd used on the marshal and hung them out to dry. When she'd done that, she prepared two more loaves of bread and placed them in the fireplace oven. Too much nervous energy left.

She took Dawg and walked over to the livery, heading for the stall that housed the marshal's horse.

Burley approached her. "Been taking real good care of that horse," he said.

"I see that." She took a good look at him. He was steady on his feet and his eyes were clear. Apparently someone had put the fear of God in him. "Someone might come looking for Mac or the marshal. Jake and Ike are keeping watch at the pass. They may need your help."

"I'll do anything. Mr. Mac, he said he would take me with you when you go." He looked at her with pleading eyes. "I can still go with you…?"

She nodded. "Just don't sleep on your watch, and don't take a drink. If you see any riders approach, get back here as fast as you can."

"I swear, Miss Sam," he said.

She peeked in on the marshal on her return and saw he was sleeping.

A farmer. The marshal had been a farmer before going to war. What had changed him into a man hunter? He said he'd lost a home. Did he have a family? A wife waiting for him? Children?

Somehow she didn't think so. Yet the possibility sent an odd pang through her.

She closed the door. Archie would be hungry. She hoped Mac would be, as well. He'd eaten next to nothing since he'd arrived. Just a spoonful of broth now and then.

She realized she was trying to think of anything but the marshal and how inexplicably she was drawn to him. *Inexplicably.* Another Reese word. Now she fully understood its meaning.

Stop daydreaming. She climbed the stairs to Mac's room.

Mac opened his eyes when she walked in. They weren't as bloodshot as they had been. He tried to lift himself up on one arm, and the strain showed in his face. "Sam," he said with a ghost of a smile.

She grinned at him. "You're feeling better."

He looked down at his bandaged hand and gave her a wry smile. "Looks like...my gun-fighting days are over."

"You wanted that for a long time."

"Not this way."

"Can't go back now."

"No," he admitted.

She felt his cheek. Still warm. Too warm. But not as hot as it had been. "Do you think you can eat something? Jake gave us some venison, and I made a stew."

"Sounds good."

Archie jerked awake. He looked at her, then at Mac. He slowly got to his feet.

"He's better," she said.

Archie nodded. "The fever broke. All those poultices you made."

A rare compliment from him.

Mac winked at her. It wasn't as good as his usual winks, but given the fact she'd thought she might lose him just hours earlier, it looked real good.

"You're still a...sight for sore eyes," Mac said, each word an effort.

To him, maybe, but he was prejudiced. She'd never cared much about her appearance.

Now for the briefest of moments, she wished she'd taken a little more interest.

Damn the marshal a thousand times over.

She turned her attention back to Mac. It would be at least

another day before he could stand. Probably two, and another before he could maneuver downstairs.

And the marshal? How long before he would be well enough to cause a problem?

"I'll bring you something to eat," she said. "And a shot of whiskey."

"Burley...hasn't drunk it all yet?"

"We kept some hidden from him."

"Is Reese back?" Mac asked.

Sam exchanged looks with Archie. "No. He should be here any day."

"We need...to get started. You need...your chance. Not isolated up here with a bunch of old men."

"I like being isolated up here with a bunch of old men," she retorted.

She earned a bigger grin, and swooped down and hugged him. "I'm so glad you're better."

There must have been something in the hug, because his eyes changed. Searched hers. "You seem...different."

She went cold inside. Was it that obvious? Had one kiss changed her? "I'm just glad to see you're better," she said, her gaze avoiding Archie's. "And I'm ready to go as soon as you are."

"Soon," he said. "A lot sooner than that old worrier, Archie, says."

She prayed Mac was right, now that there was a new urgency. They had all hoped Mac had been forgotten, that the law had lost interest. That folly was gone now.

"I know," she said. "I'm getting everything ready. We'll leave as soon as you can travel. Reese can join us later."

"Don't...want you hurt." Mac looked so tired it scared her. He'd always been strong and sure.

So was the marshal. The two men shared a similar presence. The kind that sent most people scurrying away. The aura of danger, of untamed vitality, oozed from both.

Archie muttered under his breath as if he could read her very thoughts.

"I'd better get the stew," she said, and started for the stairs before he did.

She hurried downstairs but realized quickly that she wasn't going to avoid a conversation. Archie was behind her. "Now Mac's on the mend, we won't be able to keep him up here long."

"I know," she whispered. "What will he do if he finds the marshal?"

"I have no damned idea. Can't figure him anymore. Don't know why he felt it was so all-fired important to take the gold to Denver himself."

"He was restless," she replied. But that wasn't the real reason. Mac knew Archie's rheumatism was painful. It would be bad enough on the trip north. He didn't want to subject Archie to a trip to Denver, as well. Yet they would need cash along the way.

Archie shrugged. "Don't matter none now. What's done is done. And now the law and others probably know we're here." His wrinkled face softened as he studied her. "I ain't gonna let anyone take Mac."

She suddenly realized she hadn't told him about Benson. It was a sign of how the marshal confused her.

"I asked the marshal about who was after Mac. Name is Benson, Calhoun Benson. He said Mac killed Benson's son. He's hiring gunslingers."

Archie's face creased into a worried frown, and she realized he knew the name. "You're sure."

She nodded. "You know him?"

"Ran into him a few years ago when I was carrying freight. Had a load for him. He tried to cheat me. Then threatened me. But, like some big men, he was a coward. Remember the kid, as well. Kept egging his pa on. Mean and sneaky as a snake, but his pa doted on him."

"Then you think the marshal told the truth?"

"Could be. Don't think Benson would come alone, but I can sure see him sending others."

She told him about her conversation with Jake. "They'll

watch the pass, let us know if anyone's coming. If they do, we should have time to hide in one of the old mines. I have one picked out and I'll take some supplies there tomorrow."

"Don't like the idea of hiding. Could get trapped there, but Mac ain't ready to ride yet." He grabbed two bowls, ladled the stew into them and went upstairs before she could answer. Dawg went with him, his nose following the food.

Sam looked toward the marshal's room. Tempted. She was tempted every minute of every hour. No, she told herself. She had work to do. She spent the afternoon piling supplies on a table. Blankets. Matches. A lantern. Then food. Definitely the jerky and hardtack. They couldn't take much. Just as much as the animals could carry in addition to their riders. Montana. She wanted everything to be ready the moment Mac could ride. And they would have to avoid most towns.

Would the marshal be riding after them?

She prepared another poultice for him. She wanted to check the wound, to make sure there was no infection, although she saw the irony in it. She was working to repair him, knowing that her success might well come back to haunt her.

She'd just finished when she heard a muffled yell from the marshal's room. She hesitated, then grabbed the key and entered. He was tossing in the bed, his eyes closed.

His words were unintelligible. Sarah again? The woman apparently hovered in his nightmares.

Sam approached the bed and leaned down. Light filtered through from the main room and she saw that his face was wet. Sweat or tears? She didn't know what to do. Wake him? Or leave him tortured by nightmares?

Don't get too close to him!

That didn't matter now. She had to do something. She'd never seen such pain. Not physical, but gut-wrenching. It came from deep inside.

It was dangerous waking a sleeping man, particularly one who lived a violent life. She owed him nothing, but she couldn't watch anyone in that much pain.

"Marshal," she said in a soft voice.

The thrashing continued, and so did the agony in his voice as he repeated, "Sarah."

She touched him on the shoulder, prepared to move back quickly if necessary. Instead, he quieted. He opened his eyes and stared at her as if he'd never seen her before. His breathing was labored. His dark eyes were red rimmed.

They slowly focused on her. His tense body gradually relaxed.

Archie had urged her to keep her distance. If he was feigning weakness, he could still grab her. He might be strong enough. But he couldn't go more than a step, and her gun was in the other room. She touched his forehead. Hot.

"You called out."

"Sorry…to disturb you," he said in a tone that clearly implied he wasn't sorry at all.

"You called out for 'Sarah' several times."

His face hardened and she felt a new jolt in her stomach.

A muscle flexed in his throat again. It was the only way she knew when she'd struck a nerve.

"Who is Sarah?" She knew she shouldn't ask. Shouldn't take any kind of interest in him, but she couldn't resist.

His face froze. "My wife."

Wife? She hadn't expected that. "She must miss you."

"She's dead," he said flatly.

She didn't know how to reply to that. She wished she hadn't asked, but now that she had, she decided to continue. "Will you tell me about her?"

He closed his eyes, and she thought she'd lost him, that he had drawn away into a dark place.

Then he opened them. "She and I married at seventeen," he said. "We were neighbors and…friends since we both could walk. I built a farm on some acreage in Kansas my father owned. And when the war started, I enlisted."

She saw his hand wrap around the side of the iron bed. She wanted to reach out and touch him, but she knew from his face he wouldn't want that. Not now. He had something to say, and he was going to say it his way.

"My brother stayed home. That was the agreement. I would go and my brother would watch over our farms. I didn't know when I left that Sarah was with child. I didn't know it until a year later when the mail caught up with me. We had a daughter." She heard guilt in his voice. Guilt and rage and sorrow.

"When I came home from war, all I found were three graves and a burned-out house. Southern renegades had raped and murdered her, and murdered my child and brother. There was no one left except my sister-in-law, who was teaching school in town."

She instinctively put her hand on his. Tears stung the back of her eyes. "I'm so sorry," she said. Her heart cried for him, for the young soldier who returned home to unspeakable violence.

"And that," he said quietly, "is how I went from being farmer to a marshal. I hunted down the animals who killed Sarah. And I continue to hunt for Emma's killer."

"It isn't Mac," she said.

"Others say he's the one. A trial will decide."

His voice was hard again. As hard as the stone on the mountain. As unforgiving. She knew why he'd told her the story. He was not going to give up his quest for Mac.

Warning given. Warning taken.

She wasn't sure what to do next. Or say. She ached for him. She ached for Mac. She ached for herself.

She resorted to medicine. "I have a fresh poultice," she said, "and I want to see how the wound is coming."

Not waiting for an answer, she took off the old one. She washed the wound, being as gentle as she could, then put the new poultice on. "It looks good," she said, glancing up at him.

He was staring at her. "You do that well."

"Archie taught me well."

"Where's the old man?" he asked gruffly.

"He's around."

"And MacDonald. Would he approve?"

"I don't know."

She saw the doubt in his eyes. He was still trying to figure out the relationships.

"I think not," he muttered, answering his own question.

She decided to change the subject. "I made some stew. Can you eat?"

He nodded.

She left and quickly returned with a tin plate, setting it on the table. She'd already cut the meat in small pieces and mostly filled the plate with the thick broth.

She leaned over him and helped him to a sitting position. The air was combustible as skin touched skin. He was wearing the shirt again, but it was unbuttoned and the now familiar ribbons of tingling warmth surged through her.

Archie would not be happy if he knew she was touching the marshal, that she was this close to him. Close enough that she heard his heart beat. Close enough that the heat of his chest radiated through hers. Radiated and burned. She moved away as if scalded.

Her hand was unsteady as she picked up the plate and spoon. She'd purposely not brought a fork. "I'll feed you," she said, pulling the chair over to sit on. "You'll never balance the plate on that wounded leg, Marshal."

"Jared. My name is Jared."

She knew that. She knew it from the possessions she'd found in his saddlebags. She hadn't wanted to use it. Too intimate. But that horse was already out of the barn. In fact, they were wrapped in intimacy.

"You should know it if you're going to feed me," he persisted. His voice sounded stronger. She wondered if he was pretending to be more ill than he was. But no, she'd seen similar wounds. She knew the effects of horrific pain and the kind of loss of blood he'd suffered.

"Jared, then." She offered him a bite of stew and he ate it. She watched as he chewed, then he stared at her quizzically.

"Is there anything you can't do?"

"Yes."

He looked perplexed when she didn't continue, but she wasn't planning to list her shortcomings.

He ate the stew then. Slow but steady. Because he needed the strength to go after his quarry. To go after Mac.

Conflict raged inside her. She wanted him to get better. She wanted Mac to live.

When he finished, she placed the plate on the table and gave him a cup of water.

"Who is Reese?" he asked.

That surprised her. She'd hoped he'd forgotten about Reese.

"You want to go after him, too?" she shot back.

"Should I?" he asked.

"No."

"This is a hell of a place to raise a girl. Thornton didn't do you any favors." It was as if he wanted to blank out what he had told her earlier, the bitter words that had obviously cost him much.

"What do you know about it?"

"I know you shouldn't be hidden away in this sad excuse for a town." He paused, then added, "I bet you would be real fine looking in a frock."

For the first time in years, she wished she was pretty and feminine like some of the girls she'd seen in magazines. She'd worn dresses as a young girl, but as her body began to fill out, Archie thought she would be safer in the mining town if she looked more like a lad. She'd grown used to the comfort of soft cotton shirts and pants, and boots were far better in the often muddy streets than regular women's shoes. That would all change in Montana, she knew, but for the time being she was satisfied.

"How many others live in Gideon's Hope?"

The question brought her back to the man in the bed. "A few." She didn't want to offer any information that would help him. "Are you finished?" she asked, reaching for his cup.

"I need more water." His voice was silky now, and he held the cup in his lap.

She forced herself to stand. She took the cup and went over to the pitcher and poured more water. As she handed it to him, his fingers brushed hers, and the heat from his body flowed through her. The air between them was suddenly thick with tension.

Prickly shivers ran up and down her spine, turning to a raw, ragged heat she felt all the way to her toes.

She bit her lip, forced herself to move away, but the heat went with her. "I'll...I'll get Archie if you...need anything else."

She reached for the cup, and his free hand grabbed her wrist and pulled her down to him. "I meant what I said about Benson. You should get out of here."

"And you? What should we do with you?" she challenged.

"I can't come after you. Not now."

"But you will."

His clasp grew tighter and she was drawn toward him. Her wrist burned from his touch yet she didn't pull away, couldn't control the violent storm encompassing both of them. And, most frightening to her, she didn't want to.

His body was hard under hers, though she tried not to touch his wounded leg. She felt a tensing under her, and frissons of sensation ran riot through her. Wild, runaway emotions. And pounding need. Her face brushed his bristled cheek. Then his lips touched hers. Hard and angry.

She tried to twist away but couldn't. He was so much stronger than she thought. Worse, she found herself suddenly responding. Her lips softened for his, and the anger in him turned to hunger. Or was it she who was hungry? She should protest. Jerk away. Instead, the kiss deepened and his tongue plundered her mouth. She had no will of her own. Her skin was alive with feeling, with wanting.

His left hand moved sensuously across the front of her shirt, and even through the material, she felt the fire of his touch. It seeped through her skin until it reached the core of her, taunting, teasing, arousing...

Her leg touched his wounded one, and for the fleetest of

seconds he stilled. She felt shivers in him as the pain flared, but he didn't let go, and his lock on her arm was like a shackle.

She felt his arousal against her tight britches and that ignited more explosions. She'd never known a craving so strong, a need so great.

He's the enemy.

But, sweet Lucifer, how she wanted him.

Then she looked up and saw bemused intent in his eyes, and the heat suddenly turned to ice.

What was she doing?

He let go and she stumbled backward. She regained her balance and stood, dazed. Her legs were weak, and her heart thundered.

He looked as stunned as she felt. A muscle flexed in his neck. "Get the hell out of here," he said. His words were raspy, intense. "There's nothing more dangerous than hired guns after a bounty. They won't care who gets in the way."

She stared at him for a long time. He wasn't lying. "You care, Marshal?" she asked, raising one of her eyebrows as she'd seen him do.

"I don't want to see any woman caught in a crossfire," he said as his features darkened.

"I can take care of myself," she said.

"Not against a pack of killers."

She couldn't answer that. What he didn't know was the reason why she couldn't leave.

She swallowed hard. "You need some sleep," she said. "I...I have to help Archie." She heard the tremor in her voice and hoped that he attributed it to his warning and not the reaction of her body to his. He must think her wanton. She *felt* wanton.

And, now, she felt afraid.

But more of him than Benson. He might come with guns, but he wouldn't take her soul. She was bitterly afraid this man would.

8

SAM STOPPED outside the room. Heat still churned inside her. Her fingers tingled from his touch. Her breasts were swollen, and strained against her shirt. Her heart…her heart was pounding in her chest.

She wondered whether her mother had ever felt like this. Had she experienced this clawing need inside? The hot rush of blood through her veins? Had she allowed a few magical moments in the arms of a man to govern her life?

Sam recalled how happy her mother had been when Mac was in town. She wore her best dresses and took her time braiding her hair and pinning it up.

She wished her mother was still alive. She knew so little about what was happening inside her. She'd always believed love and sex went together. But she didn't love the marshal, and he made the earth shake under her.

She didn't even like him. She didn't like his profession. She didn't like the cool, enigmatic expression that gave so little away. Most of all, she didn't like the fact that he was dedicated to arresting the person she loved most in the world.

He was hard and arrogant and unbending.

Except, she admitted, for those few minutes when he'd talked about Sarah. His Sarah. It had been obvious that he'd loved her and his child. She'd ached for him then. For a moment, she'd even felt close to him. She understood what it was like to grieve.

But shared grief didn't explain why she was so attracted to the marshal. *To Jared.* She tried to tell herself it was because she had grown to womanhood, and there had been no eligible males in her life. Maybe she'd just been ready, and anyone—or almost anyone—would have raised the same sensations.

She doubted that, too. She wished she could talk to Mac, but of course that was impossible. And Archie? He would probably go kill the marshal. Only Reese might understand, and he wasn't here.

No, this was something she had to figure out on her own. *Blazes, but her heart still pounded.*

Even worse, the beguiling feelings inside had started to build on each other. She'd had one kiss, and she wanted more. Then she'd felt his body, and she wanted even more. When his hands had touched her breasts, she wanted him to touch all of her. But why did he ignite such fires in her belly?

Worse, why did she let him?

She was strong. She did her share around the saloon and panned the creek for gold. It was hard work, much harder than would-be miners had anticipated. She'd thought Jared would be weak after losing so much blood, but it had been an iron hand that drew her to him.

She should have known. She should have learned from the first time he kissed her. She never should have gotten that close to him again. And she could have stopped him at any time; all she had to do was strike his wounded leg. Instead she'd tried to avoid it, and she'd responded in a way that shamed her. It was a betrayal of Mac.

Sam's face warmed at the memory of Jared's kiss, at the feel of his hands on her and his lips...

She tried to stop trembling. *Take a step.* She couldn't let Archie see her like this. She was horrified at her reactions to the marshal. She *had* to think of him as the man who wanted to see her best friend hanged, not a man who had aroused such unfamiliar and irresistible feelings in her.

When she'd lowered her guard, he had pounced. But she couldn't blame it all on him. She had allowed it to happen.

Do something useful. She needed to finish getting supplies together in case they had to move quickly to a mine shaft or, even better, head on to Montana.

She stopped at the kitchen and used water from the pump to dampen her cheeks, then went upstairs to her room. She would have to leave some of her most prized possessions behind, particularly the medical books Reese had found. She chose one on anatomy and put it on her bed. She hoped that Reese could arrange for the other books to be shipped to wherever they settled. Then she picked up her guitar and sat on the bed. She strummed a few chords. That had to go with her.

She hadn't played since Mac's return. She'd been too busy for one thing, and too heartsick for another. But now he was getting better, she would play for him.

And the marshal. She remembered the book in his saddle-bags. A rare thing, she thought, for a lawman to carry around. Did he like music, as well? He seemed too austere for that. Now that he was awake more often, she should give his book to him.

She went up to Mac's room and called Archie to step outside. "His wound looks good. I'm going to take him some stew."

"He polite to you?" Archie asked.

She nodded.

"Didn't make any advances? Try to convince you of somethin'?"

"He just mentioned that Benson again. Said we should leave."

He muttered a string of oaths. She caught enough words to guess he was running through his army vocabulary. When he finished, he said, "You go ahead and take supplies to the mine."

"I want to see Mac first." She turned and opened the door.

Dawg lazily got to his feet from his place next to the bed. He licked her hand as if sensing she was out of sorts. She gave him a big hug before he returned to play sentinel beside Mac.

Mac was still awake. He gave her a weak smile. "Princess. You sure look better than Archie. He's been like an old woman, fussing over me like I was half-dead."

"You were," she replied. "You still are." She went to his side. She remembered how he'd looked ten years ago. He seldom joked and rarely smiled, but he'd been handsome as the devil, her mother used to say. She remembered how her mother had lit up like a star whenever he came in the door. He couldn't be much more than ten years older than the marshal, but his light brown hair was touched with gray, and in the past few days the lines in his face had deepened.

"Help me sit up," he said.

She wanted to. She wanted him to regain his strength. But not too fast. Not so fast that he would find the marshal.

How ironic that both were recovering from bullet wounds, these two enemies who were totally unaware that the other was just feet away. She and Archie had to keep it that way, at least until Mac could travel.

"I take Archie's side this time," she said. "You were barely conscious a day ago, and you won't be going anywhere if you try to do more than you should."

"This coming from the most impatient young lady I know?" he said, even as he slowly relaxed.

"I just want you to get better."

"Getting anxious to leave now?" he said with the semblance of a smile.

"I'm happy wherever you and Reese and Archie are."

"I hear Montana is a good place for cattle. Wide-open with great grazing land. We'll have a good life there."

There was real enthusiasm in his voice, and it warmed her heart. He knew his gun hand was injured. He would never have the movement needed for a quick draw, and he seemed almost relieved. She wanted to ask him about the woman mentioned by the marshal, but she couldn't. Then he would ask why she was interested. Besides, she didn't believe the marshal.

"I wish we could leave today," she said. Getting a good

distance from the marshal was not only wise but absolutely necessary.

"That's a change," he said. "I thought we would have to pry you away."

She was saved from an answer by Archie's return. "I'll stay with Mac," he said.

"I don't need anyone to stay with me," Mac protested.

"Mebbe not, but make an old man happy," Archie said.

He followed Sam out of the room, closing the door behind him. "That marshal won't need nothing else tonight," he said. "I locked the door. Now you take Dawg and get some sleep. Tomorrow, you take them supplies to the mine. If anyone comes, we'll have to move mighty fast."

She nodded. It might be the last sleep she would get for a while.

If she even could sleep. Her mind was whirling with tempestuous emotions. So was her body. Just thinking about the marshal created warm, pulsing feelings inside.

"Come," she told Dawg, who had followed her.

She went to her room down the hall and closed the door. *Don't think about him. Think about Montana. About a green valley and a herd of cattle. And peace.*

Sam went to the window and looked out. The night was dark. Clouds hurried across the sky, curtaining any light from the moon and stars. No one would be traveling tonight, not across the treacherous passes. Mac was safe for the moment. Maybe it would rain again tomorrow. The weather might give them a few more days.

But how many?

SAM ROSE at sunrise the next day. She stretched, then brushed the curtains away and stared at the rain turning the road outside into a sea of mud. Thank God.

She'd slept lightly through the night. Thunder had jerked her awake several times and the respite in between was haunted by forbidden memories of what had occurred in the room downstairs. Of all the men in the world, the marshal should be the least likely to stir such vivid and erotically painful feelings. She'd read about erotic, but she'd never thought she would feel anything like it.

She was frightened by how much she wanted to go to his room again, to engage in verbal combat as well as...

Was the door downstairs still locked? Was the marshal better? Was Mac improving by the hour? And what would happen when the two men met?

And what would happen the next time she saw the marshal? Jared? Would there be fireworks and challenge and, hell's blazes, raw, naked lust?

Lust. Now she knew what the word meant. It was no longer just an abstract notion in a book.

She started to dress. A clean pair of pants and cotton shirt, but old, worn boots. She stopped halfway through dressing and looked at herself in the full-length mirror that Reese had brought from Denver.

Always before she'd just taken a quick glance, or sometimes no glance at all. But now...she examined herself in a different way. Her hair curled around a rather ordinary face. She usually ran a comb through it in the morning. Now she wished she hadn't asked Archie to cut it every few months when it got long enough to be a bother. She was taller than most. Her father had almost reached to the sky. At least that was how it seemed to a six-year-old girl. Her mother said he was the tallest man she'd ever seen.

And now she—Sam—would be twenty-one in a month. Most girls were married by now. But she knew she wasn't the usual respectable young lady. She could cheat at poker, use a whip to slash bark off a tree and shoot bottles in the air.

A shudder ran through her at how close she'd come to killing a man. Of being killed herself. As much as she hated to admit it, if Jared had not hesitated that fraction of a second, she would probably be dead.

That meant she owed him.

She went downstairs to the kitchen and made coffee, then mixed up some biscuits and put them in the oven.

The door of the marshal's room beckoned, but she resisted. Instead she took coffee up to Mac. She knocked and entered when there was no response. Mac was alone on the bed. She hadn't heard Archie go down the stairs. He was probably planning to check on the marshal's wound and help him with personal needs. Maybe he thought now that Mac was a little better, he ought to care for the marshal himself. Maybe he'd noticed something about her had changed.

She *felt* different. Very different.

She started to leave when Mac opened his eyes.

"Sam?"

She went over to his side. "I brought you some coffee."

"What's going on?" he asked.

"What do you mean?"

"You've never been a good liar," he said slowly. His eyes were clearer than they had been. "Something is going on. Archie's acting strange. He's not telling me something. He's edgy, and that's not like him."

She wished she knew what Archie had said. Maybe part of the truth would do. "We may have to move you," she said. "A rider came by and said a posse might be coming after you."

He closed his eyes for a moment. "You can never escape the past," he said. "I thought…"

"Apparently one of the men you shot had important relatives. Jake and Ike are keeping watch at the pass. We're planning to move you to one of the old mines."

He struggled to sit upright. "I'll… We can leave for Montana now."

"Archie says you wouldn't get more than a few miles. You were nearly dead when you made it here."

"I'm not going to let you get involved."

"I'm as involved as anyone can be," she said. "You took care of me for years."

"And I can still make decisions for myself, missy."

Missy. He hadn't called her that in a long time, and only used it when she'd displeased him.

"No, you can't," she said sharply. "If you try, you'll be dead inside of two days. You still have some infection in you. You can't ride for long, and if we're caught in the open, we'll all die because we won't leave you behind and we won't give you up."

He looked stunned at her vehemence.

"Best thing you can do is stay still and get well. Faster you get better, sooner we can leave." She sat next to him, took his hand and leaned against him as she did when she was a child. "Promise me you will stay in bed. Jake and Ike are keeping watch. I'm getting a mine ready if we need it. We can all hide there for a few days."

His eyes softened. "What have we done to you, Samantha? You should be married with children, not hiding in a mine with a wanted outlaw."

Samantha? He never called her Samantha.

"Promise?" she insisted. "Eat. And rest. Promise me you won't wander around. You need as much strength as possible so we can leave for Montana when…"

His shoulders slumped, but she knew she'd won. For the moment, at least.

Maybe she should tell him about the marshal. But then she didn't know what would happen. Mac would probably go down and try to confront him, and he was no match now for even a wounded marshal.

"Yes, missy," he said obediently. "You've become mighty bossy."

"I had good teachers. Now sleep."

He lay down, but she didn't believe he'd conceded so easily. He sensed she hadn't told him everything. She wanted to stay, but she had to take supplies to the mine.

If anyone was spotted from the top of the pass, she figured they would have about an hour. She'd already taken pains to wash or burn anything with bloodstains. Hopefully the rain would continue and wipe away their tracks. If not, well, she knew a few tricks.

And the marshal? They could just leave him chained to the bed. Let him believe they had left the valley.

Blast the man.

She went down to the bar and checked the bundles she'd prepared. She added candles, turpentine and moss, along with a few pans. They might need supplies for a week or longer. By the time she finished, she had filled four large flour sacks.

Keep busy. Keep away from the marshal. He's nothing but trouble.

She couldn't help glance at his room, though. Maybe he needed some breakfast.

Then the door opened, and Archie came out. He closed the door behind him but didn't lock it.

"How is the marshal?" she asked.

Archie shrugged. "He'll live to hunt again. Too bad." He paused, then added, "He's getting better too quick. Constitution of a damned horse. I chained him to the bed with his cuffs. If he got past you, I wouldn't be surprised if he crawled up them stairs."

Sam agreed. She knew exactly how strong he was. "Did you take him any breakfast?"

"Took some hardtack. He doesn't need anything fancy. Ornery bastard."

"You always said good food speeds healing."

"You want 'im to heal fast?"

She had no answer to that. "I saw Mac. He's better."

"Not as much as he thinks," Archie grumped.

"I talked him into staying put for a while."

Archie pointed to the sacks on the table. "Got everything there?"

She nodded. "Blankets. Bacon, beans, coffee, lots of hardtack and jerky. I tore up another sheet for bandages, and I added a bottle of whiskey. Some jars of preserves and cans of fruit. I think my horse and your mule can take it all in one trip."

He nodded. "I'll take Mac's horse and pick up Burley. We'll meet Jake at the pass. Best Burley don't see you going toward the mines. A drink of whiskey, and he'll talk forever."

"Mac might try to come downstairs with neither of us here."

"I don't think he can get out of bed yet." He hesitated, then added, "If you go in that room, Sam, be careful. There's something in that man's eyes.... He ain't gonna give up."

She hoped her face hadn't flamed again. He didn't know how careful she needed to be. She felt Archie's eyes on her. They seemed to see everything.

He shifted on his feet and grumbled again. "The marshal's still in a lot of pain, and it should be a few days before he can put weight on that leg, but..." His voice trailed off. "I warned him. He tries anything with you, and I'll whip the skin from his hide. Don't care who or what he is."

She waited as Archie found some oilcloth and helped her wrap up the filled flour sacks. "Leave after you see me ride out with Burley," he said.

When they finished to his satisfaction, he gave her a long look. "If this Benson or more law comes," he said slowly, "we'll have a problem with the marshal."

She stiffened. "What do you mean?"

"I might have to kill him," Archie said flatly. "We can't take him with us to the mine—he'd be too much trouble with that leg. If we leave him here, he would tell anyone who came that we'd just left and that'd start an extensive search."

"But..."

"It's simple, Sam. The marshal's gaining strength. How long could we keep him silent in a mine?"

He looked her straight in the eyes. "If he's right and Benson brings an army of gunmen, it'll come down to Mac or the marshal."

THE WORDS CHILLED HER, but she tried not to let it show. She knew Archie meant what he said. He and Mac went way back.

He'd spoken the words so easily. Yet they stabbed her like a knife in the stomach. Her reaction was ridiculous, she knew. She could have killed the marshal the day he came looking for Mac. She'd taken that risk. Now the possibility of his death was excruciating.

Maybe Archie was testing her. Or maybe he was preparing her. Worry haunted his eyes when he looked at her now. She was still a child to him. It was as if he was testing her, weighing what she would do. Then he nodded. "You'll do okay, girl." He left without another word.

She wondered whether he sensed what had happened between her and the marshal yesterday. Did he suspect how much faster her heart beat when she was around their captive? How her body was experiencing totally new feelings and needs?

Maybe she could make a deal with the marshal. They would let him go, and he would forget about Mac.

Except he would never agree. She didn't know him that well, but deep in her soul she knew. It wasn't in the man.

She had to try, anyway. She poured coffee into a tin cup, buttered some of the newly baked biscuits and added honey.

She hesitated. Was this only an excuse to see him? To test whether she could forget about last night? That it had been a temporary—monumental—lapse in judgement? She just knew she wanted to see him. Had to see him.

He was awake when she unlocked his door, but she knew he would be, since Archie had been in there.

He was halfway sitting, his upper body resting against the iron framework of the bed. He wore a shirt, but it was unbuttoned and open. And now his right wrist was encircled by iron. The other end was locked around the iron bedpost. The chain itself was about three feet long, which gave him some movement.

His hawklike eyes were inscrutable as she studied him. The sheet only partially covered his lower half. She noticed instantly that Archie had provided him with a clean pair of long johns— probably Mac's. The right leg of the underwear was partially cut off to provide access to the wound.

The long johns were tight on him. He was heavier than Mac, and taller, and they sculpted his body, making the mound at the apex of his thighs even more obvious. She averted her eyes but not before a burning ache took hold in her stomach.

Lord help her, but he was pure, powerful masculinity, and

the cuff around his wrist only served to emphasize rather than diminish it.

"Ah, I hoped you would come," he said with a slight—very slight—smile.

Archie was right. He *was* better.

She handed the cup of coffee to him and watched as he sipped it. Then she rested the plate on his lap, only too aware that the mound underneath the sheet was bigger than when she came in.

He followed her gaze. "I need help again," he said. He pulled on the chain. "I'm somewhat inconvenienced."

"You seem pretty good at managing things," she said. "There's plenty of room on the plate for that coffee."

"But if I spill it…?"

Damn him. She could envision the hot coffee spilling over his…

She snatched the plate back. "I'll just hold it until you finish the coffee, then you can eat."

"I think I would prefer it the other way around."

He was deliberately aggravating her. She was ready to take both coffee and biscuits away when his expression softened, revealing that damn dimple. "I've been smelling those biscuits all morning."

Sam gave him the plate and held the coffee. She watched as he used his free hand to grab a biscuit. He took a bite, then looked up. "You made these?"

She nodded.

"I'm impressed."

He took another bite of biscuit and chewed slowly. Maybe too slowly. Even that small act was…titillating.

She pulled the chair closer to him and put the coffee on it. He could darn well help himself.

"Don't go," he said.

"I have work to do."

"I suppose I should apologize to you for yesterday."

"But you won't."

"No. I would be lying. You felt too good."

"It must have hurt you. Or you're stronger than you pretend…" She allowed the word to dangle.

"Maybe *inspired* is a better word."

"Why don't I believe that?" she replied. She'd never bantered with a man before, certainly not when there was such a sensual overtone. She didn't know the rules.

His gaze caught hers. "It's true."

"I don't like marshals," she replied sharply. She had to do something before he lured her back into the sensual web again. *Do something. Say something. Anything to break the spell.*

"I figured that out."

"I tried to kill you," she said. "I can still do it."

"Would you?" he said, his voice low and intimate. "You didn't seem to try that hard the first time."

"I missed," she lied.

"I don't think so. You're not a killer."

"Do you want to bet your life on it?"

He took several more sips of coffee, held the cup out for her to take, then took another bite of biscuit. Honey coated his lips. That half smile was there again.

The exquisite heat that had so undermined her yesterday flowed back though her veins. Or maybe it had never left. It had just been lying deep inside, ready to flare even stronger.

"Coffee," he said, holding out his free left hand. He looked at her with innocence in his face, but she feared he was laughing inside. She was acting like a besotted fool. But then she'd never felt like this before. There was a fever inside her and the cure was just feet away.

When she handed him the cup, she was mortified that her hand shook slightly, and even more mortified at her disappointment that he didn't grab her again.

"Tell me about Thornton." His voice was soft, insistent.

"You already know everything," she retorted. "So you say."

"I'm willing to listen. I don't have anything else to do right now." Despite the mild words, his eyes simmered with challenge.

"He's nothing like you say."

"Your Archie said he helped take care of you. Why?"

"Why what?"

"Did he take care of you? He's not related, is he?"

"He loved my mother," she said simply.

"And your mother?" he persisted. "Did she love him?"

She nodded. "He feared that his...reputation would put her in danger. Does that sound like a vicious outlaw?" she asked defiantly.

He wanted to say something to her defense of Thornton. She saw it in his face, but he didn't immediately reply.

"He's lived here a long time, then?" he asked after a lengthy pause.

"Why does that matter?"

"Because it's said he's committed robberies in the past few years. Maybe he had help."

She tried to hide her disquiet. What if he went after Archie or Reese, as well? "You believe everything that's said?"

"No, but I look into it." He paused. "Who looks after you when he's gone? That old man?"

"That old man can whip the skin off your hide." She clamped her mouth shut. She was talking too much. Yet she wanted to convince him to go away. That Mac wasn't the heartless killer he was after.

"And," she added, "I don't need anyone to look after me. I take care of myself. Have for a long time."

"What about schooling?" He paused, then added in an intimate tone, "Doesn't it get lonely?"

"My education was probably as good as yours," she retorted. "I know Latin. And history. Astronomy. I know about herbs and medicine. I probably know as much as you in book learning—more, most likely."

"The old man knows Latin? Or Thornton?" He sounded skeptical.

"You don't know anything about him—or about me." She clenched her teeth together. She had to leave before he wormed out any more. Before she melted under the deep gaze of his eyes and the heat that lurked there. One thing, for sure, she wasn't going to mention Reese. That would only give the marshal another target.

She looked at the coffee cup. It was empty. She filled it with water. "I have to go," she said.

"I had a book in my saddlebags," he said. "I would...be grateful if you'd bring it to me."

Grateful? Not a word he'd used before. But she imagined he was bored with nothing to do but feel the pain she'd inflicted on him. The reminder stung.

She nodded. Reading would keep him busy while she was gone.

She had left the saddlebags behind the bar. She fetched the book and returned, handing it to him.

"Why do you stay here?" he asked suddenly. "You're pretty and..."

That *pretty* word again. He threw it around too easily.

"Isn't there any place you love?" she asked softly. "Anyone at all you love?"

His face turned to stone again. The warm room suddenly became frigid. She pulled the chair close to him so she could leave the coffee cup within reach. Then she added a pitcher of fresh water.

He said nothing, and his eyes were hooded. She wanted to reach out and touch him. She yearned to do that. But he turned away from her, and she left, knowing she had done nothing to help Mac. And not that much for the marshal.

Nor—she realized—had she done anything to quench the burning, untamed need inside her. Instead, she'd only added fuel to it.

9

JARED YANKED at the chain binding him to the bed.

It had been an hour or so since Sam left. The door was heavy, too heavy to hear any conversations outside. The book lay beside him unopened.

He tried to shift himself up in the bed to get better leverage, but his leg still hurt like the devil, and even that small effort drained him.

Another part of his anatomy hurt, as well, and that particularly galled him.

He managed to get to a sitting position at last. He probably could have done so earlier, but he'd wanted Sam and the old man to believe him more helpless than he was. He wanted her to come close to him. He'd even been considering seducing her to find MacDonald's whereabouts.

What he hadn't expected was to become entrapped in his own scheme. He was beginning to care far too much. He waited impatiently every hour for her to come into the room so he could see the appealing vulnerability she tried to hide behind a tough veneer. He wanted to watch her cheeks flush when he touched her, by accident or on purpose. And most of all to feel her lips on his.

He hadn't expected to grow so hard, and she'd felt that hardness, all right. He'd seen the turmoil, then wonder, in those golden eyes as she'd instinctively responded.

Hell, he got hard just thinking how she'd felt against him. Despite her slender build, she'd been incredibly soft. He ached, and not only from the wound. It was altogether too long since he'd had a woman.

Problem was Sam was not just any woman. He felt like the worst kind of scoundrel to take advantage of her. And he had been doing that. At first, it had been purposeful. She had shot him, after all, and he'd felt little compunction about trying to find out what he could about MacDonald and her role in the outlaw's life. But that was when he thought she was MacDonald's woman. He knew now that she wasn't, not in the way he'd first thought.

Didn't that say something about Thornton/MacDonald?

He brushed that thought aside, and his thoughts turned back to Sam and the enigma she was. Untamed and free and unconventional. Strong and determined. And yet gentle, even tender. Wistful. Vulnerable. Quick-witted. Sam was like a thunderstorm while Sarah had been a gentle rain.

Dammit, but she touched him and excited him in ways that no woman had since his wife died. She made him feel alive for the first time since his wife and daughter died, and her presence temporarily banished the pain.

He hadn't thought anyone could touch his heart again. And certainly not a girl who dressed like a lad and shot lawmen.

Isn't there any place you love? Anyone you love?

The question had thrown him, and after she left he'd felt a loneliness he'd never permitted himself to acknowledge before. *No.* There wasn't any place he loved. No one he loved, and now he knew how empty his life was.

But nothing had really changed. She'd made it clear she wouldn't hesitate to shoot him again if he tried to take her MacDonald. And he had no intention of leaving here without the man who killed Emma.

He was nearby. Or she wouldn't have gone to such lengths to protect him.

Why hadn't Thornton come to confront him while he was

helpless? That was the question. From all accounts, the outlaw was a fast draw. One of the fastest. Was he wounded? Sick?

That was the only thing that made sense.

He studied the iron bedpost to which he was chained, but it was welded to the frame. He remembered being told the room had been used as a jail. Now he knew why. No windows. A stout door and wooden floors. A jail in a saloon. Made about as much sense as everything else in Gideon's Hope.

He then turned his attention to the interior of the room and looked for something that could help him free himself. Both the woman and the old man had been careful not to leave anything within reach except the chair, the metal pitcher and the tin cup.

Several possibilities. Maybe he could utilize the chair in some way. Use one of the legs as a lever to pry the iron bedpost free. It would be difficult with his wrist chained to it. And the chair looked flimsy. But maybe there was a scrap of metal he could use to play with the lock of the wrist irons.

He inspected the cup. No rough edge to use against the iron in the shackles. His badge? It had been on his vest, but that was gone. God knew where it was, or where his saddlebags were.

Damn, there was nothing. He would have to get something from her. A pin of some kind.

He had to get out of here for more than one reason. When he didn't report back in Denver, others would come looking for him. He had no reason to believe whoever it was wouldn't meet with the same reception he had.

And someone else might not realize Sam was a woman. Or care. His blood ran cold at the thought. He sure as hell didn't want her killed. Or the irascible Archie, either. They hadn't had to doctor him. They could have left him out in the street to bleed to death.

But chained here, he couldn't do anything to stop a bloodbath. A paid posse didn't care who got in the way.

He believed in the law. It was his life. It was the only way to stop the kind of wanton killing that had taken his family. He hated criminals, particularly those who preyed on honest, hardworking people, and he despised murderers. Thornton/MacDonald had been on the top of that list for a long time.

He wasn't ready to believe this new version of the man, nor would he dishonor his badge. Not even for a sprite of a woman who'd charmed herself into his heart.

AFTER SHE LEFT the marshal's room, Sam checked on Mac. Asleep. She thought Archie had probably given him some laudanum to keep him still while they were gone. There wasn't much left. She said a silent prayer that there would be no more injuries.

She carried the supplies out to the stable. Burley was gone, and Archie's mule was in his stall. She quickly packed the mule and her own horse and left for the mine she'd selected as a possible hideout.

She knew it well. Mac had stored some supplies there years ago in the event he might need to disappear for a while.

It was one of the larger mines. Deep but with a relatively small opening that permitted horses to enter but could be easily concealed. After the nuggets ran out in the creek, groups of miners joined their claims and used dynamite to blast into the mountains. They dreamed of finding a vein, but they never did, and eventually, one by one, the shafts were abandoned.

She didn't know how long they might have to stay—if they had to stay at all—but she figured five days for four to five people at most. She didn't know whether that total would include Reese or the marshal.

There was still the possibility that Jared had been lying. Maybe no one was coming after Mac. Maybe he thought he could scare them into surrendering Mac.

When she reached the mine, she stood there for a moment, remembering all the hopes that had gone into this shaft and others. She could almost hear the sound of dynamite blasting into the mountain. See the anxious, expectant faces. But all hope was long gone. She placed the blankets as far back as she could and protected them with oilcloth. She did the same with the food items, then stacked some wood inside for a fire. She doubted it would be used. If someone was looking for them, a fire would be a reckless indulgence.

When she was satisfied that her hoard would be protected from rain and animals, she carefully placed branches at the entrance.

It would survive a quick look if not a longer one, but then anyone from outside the area would not be likely to know about the mines. She was gambling that the bounty hunters would look in town first and then leave when they couldn't find Mac.

Which was why Burley had to come with them. Jake and Ike could easily fade into the mountains.

When she had arranged everything to her satisfaction, she rode back to the livery through heavy rain. Water leaked inside her slicker and pasted her hair to her head.

She shivered as she went inside. Mac's horse was still missing. So Archie hadn't returned yet. Neither had Burley. She unsaddled her horse and stabled Archie's mule.

Where was Archie? She didn't like him out in the rain this long. The path was slippery, and his legs gave him a lot of pain. Worry nibbled at her as she grabbed her rifle and walked rapidly to the saloon. She tossed the slicker on a chair and placed her rifle behind the bar.

The door to the marshal's room was still closed. Nothing looked amiss. Sam hurried up to Mac's room and opened the door. Chaos. Mac was on the floor, Dawg whining at his side. Shattered crockery surrounded both.

She stooped next to Mac and examined him. There was a bump on his head as well as new cuts on his good hand. His face was flush. He muttered something, then moaned. She examined Dawg briefly. His paw was bleeding from a cut.

"Mac," she said. No answer. "Mac," she repeated, this time insistently. She tugged at him, and his body jerked. His eyes opened.

"What happened?" she asked.

"Heard…something below. Dawg…he was barking. I called you and Archie…no one answered. I tried to get up…and fell. Knocked over…the damn pitcher. Must have hit my head. You were…right. I'm not strong enough…" He stopped. "Are you all right? You and…Archie?"

She nodded. "I had a few things to do."

"I called…"

She put her hand on his shoulder. Inwardly she was shaking. What was the noise he'd heard? Had the marshal escaped? Had he gone for help? He was in no position to go far. Not with that leg.

Mac was bleeding. She wasn't even going to try to lift him. He couldn't afford another fall. She put a pillow under his head. "Don't move," she directed him. "Stay," she told Dawg.

She hurried downstairs, fetched a broom and dustpan, and returned. In seconds, she'd swept up the pieces of broken crockery. Then she cleaned and bandaged two cuts and picked a piece of pottery from Dawg's paw. She would have to wait for Archie to get Mac in bed again.

"I'll be back," she promised, then ran downstairs. Two men—deadly enemies—wounded and within a few hundred feet of each other. She and Archie had been foolish to think they could keep them from finding out about each other.

She also knew who Archie would protect if a decision had to be made.

The door to the marshal's room was still closed. She heard nothing inside. Maybe he had fallen, too. Maybe that's what Mac heard. But the fact he *had* heard something meant she needed to investigate.

She ran her fingers through her damp hair, then located the key to the room. She took the Colt from her holster and fitted the key in the lock. Then she opened the door, slamming it against the inside wall in case he'd somehow gotten loose from the handcuffs and stood behind the door. The marshal was sitting up. A broken chair lay beside the bed. Half of one of its legs was on the sheets next to his book. The bedpost was slightly bent but still intact. The cuff of the irons was still locked to it, and the other remained secure around the marshal's right wrist.

She immediately knew what had happened. The marshal had managed to break the chair and tried to use one of its legs to bend the iron post. Or maybe he'd planned to hide it under the sheet and use it as a weapon. She should have known he wouldn't give up easily.

"Throw that chair leg to the other side of the room," she said.

He shrugged and obeyed. "I heard a noise upstairs," he said, a question in his eyes. Then his gaze fixed on her wrist. "You're bleeding."

She looked down. She'd been in such a hurry she hadn't noticed—or felt—the cut on her hand. She must have gotten it while handling the broken pieces of the pitcher.

It wasn't that deep, but when she turned she saw drops of blood leading from the door. She felt it now. A sting. And the blood was warm. A glance told her it was only a surface cut.

"Let me see it," he ordered.

She didn't move.

"I can't escape," he said with sudden exasperation. "I won't hurt you."

She resisted. He would use any advantage. She knew that as well as she knew the sun would rise on the morrow.

"I can take care of it," she said curtly, unsettled at how much she wanted to hold out her hand to him and have him care for it. She went outside and washed the small wound under the water pump. There were still strips of cloth on the table that Archie had left. She quickly tied one around the cut, then returned to the marshal's room.

She couldn't stay long, not with Mac awake upstairs, but she took the time to refill the metal pitcher of water and place it near him. "Looks like you went to war with the room."

"I was bored."

"Sleep would have been more beneficial," she said drily. "Or the book."

"I heard a crash above," he repeated.

"That was Archie," she said curtly.

"Was he hurt?"

"No." It was only a partial lie. Archie hadn't been hurt.

"He should be more careful."

"Like you?" she shot back.

"Like me," he confirmed, that half smile appearing again. "I thought you might return quicker if you thought I was up to mischief."

A shiver ran down her back. The noise had aroused his curiosity, and she wasn't sure he believed her explanation.

"I could use a shave," he said, touching the bristles on his face with his free hand.

She was excruciatingly aware of that. The new beard gave him an even more compelling look that was more than a little unsettling.

"I think you could use those leg irons in your saddlebags, instead," she retorted. "Maybe that would keep you still enough to heal."

He smiled slightly. Damn him. It was as if he saw inside her. All the tumbling emotions and conflicting battles. Why did he always make her feel uncertain? Unsettled? "I'm glad you care," he said finally.

"I don't," she protested. "Well, maybe I do, but only because I don't want to be responsible for someone's death. Or crippling. Doesn't matter who. I would feel the same about any critter."

"You would?"

"Even more so," she said, lifting her chin in battle. She hated the smile that was spreading to his eyes. She hated it, and yet it was…riveting. She needed to leave. Now…while she still could. His effect on her was too powerful.

"Afraid I'll kiss you again, Miss Sam?"

He was baiting her, and she realized that he had studied her, looking for a tactic that might work for him. And he'd succeeded, dammit. She was tempted to move closer to him. She wondered how it would feel to rub her hand over his face, to soap it, then use the razor across it. She had shaved Mac on occasion and had offered to shave Archie's beard. She suspected shaving the marshal would be something entirely different.

"I'm not afraid of anything, Marshal."

"Jared," he reminded her as if he had been reading her mind. It annoyed her. "Then what about the shave?"

"I might cut you."

"I'll take that chance," he said, stretching out, his body tightening under the cover.

Her stomach twisted into a hot knot. She took a steadying breath. She wasn't going to let him bait her. He was enjoying it too much. It was giving him a measure of revenge.

She approached and kicked the pieces of wood away from the bed, then picked them up. "Archie…" She stopped herself. If Archie had walked in here, no telling what he would do.

She didn't like lying to Archie, even by omission. She didn't like the marshal for making her do it. But she kept remembering Archie's words. *Kill him.* Death didn't mean that much to Archie. She'd heard his war stories. She knew he'd killed as well as healed. She thought he probably did both with the same calm expertise.

"You're a fool," she said.

"You didn't answer my question about a shave."

"It wasn't worth an answer, but if you really want one, no."

"What about a deck of cards, then?" he persisted as she moved toward the door.

She turned around.

"You play poker." It was as much question as statement.

"Some," she replied.

"What about a game?"

"What stakes?" she replied recklessly.

"Well, you have everything of mine," he said. "I don't even have clothes to barter with, except this shirt, and these long johns."

She refused to recognize the insinuation in his words. "We're not thieves," she said. "There's always your horse, your saddle, the coins in that pouch in your saddlebags." She hoped her voice was as relaxed and challenging as his own.

"Ah, you like big stakes, then?"

"Why play otherwise?" She needed to leave. Archie would be here any minute. And she should check on Mac again.

"What do you have to offer *me?*" he said lazily. "You know all my worldly belongings. What about Miss Sam's?"

"Just plain Sam will do," she corrected, just as he had corrected her.

"Doesn't exactly fit," he said, one bushy eyebrow raised. "Not the plain part, anyway." He paused, letting his words echo in the dim room. "What about letting me see you in a dress?"

She'd expected something different. Something like letting him go.

"I don't have a dress," she lied. She did have one but it was buried at the bottom of a trunk.

"That's just a pure damn shame," he said.

"Another choice?" she asked, hoping her voice wasn't trembling as much as her legs were. Why couldn't he be as old as Archie?

He gave her a speculative look. "What about eggs and bacon?"

"Unfortunately our last chicken ran into a coyote," she said. "Try again."

"Another kiss? To start."

Blood rushed to her face again, and her heart skipped a beat. Hell's bells, but she wished that didn't happen. She usually knew how to control her reactions, but this new rush of awareness went straight to her cheeks. She didn't know how to hold it in check, or the other feelings that tormented her body.

"Let's go back to you," she said. "We don't need another horse, and I don't want your money." She paused. "If I win, you forget about Mac."

"Now, I would need equal collateral," he replied. "How about you telling me where he is if I win?"

"Not bloody likely."

He raised an eyebrow. "What about information?" he offered.

She looked at him skeptically. "I told you I wouldn't talk about Mac."

"Yourself. I want to know more about you." His eyes were hooded.

"Why?"

"You intrigue me."

Probably in all the wrong ways. But still her heart tripped dangerously. She wanted to know more about him, too. The more time she spent with him, the more she wanted to know what lay behind those inscrutable eyes. "I'll take information, as well," she said. She felt confident about her skills. During winter months, Reese taught her everything he knew about poker, and last spring had taken her on one of his gambling trips. She'd been dressed as a lad, binding her breasts, and every player had thought her easy pickings, only to discover their pockets emptying. Reese had said she was a natural.

She still played with Archie, Reese and Mac, sometimes all of them at one time, and she could hold her own.

At least the marshal was no longer asking about the noise he'd heard above. She needed to keep it that way.

Her eyes went to his hand, resting beside his head. If the chain bothered him, it didn't show. But then she'd already learned that he seldom revealed any true emotion.

She wanted information she could use to bargain, maybe use against him. And he wanted the same. The challenge was irresistible, even though there were dangers. Not the least of which was her growing attraction to him. Hell's blazes, more than that. What she felt was raw, naked desire. Even worse, she was beginning to like him. Maybe even…no, not possible. Not possible at all.

Her gaze met his, but she averted her eyes before he spun more magic. Before she succumbed to it again.

10

JARED'S GAZE FOLLOWED her as she left the room. He'd expected more reaction to the broken chair. But then she'd surprised him from the moment she'd confronted him in the street.

He'd challenged her to a poker game as a last-minute ploy to keep her from leaving. He told himself the longer she stayed, the more he would learn. But the truth was he didn't want her to leave.

She lit the room with her very presence. She was such an appealing combination of grit and earnestness and loyalty that he ached in the area where his heart was located. He found himself missing her immensely when she was gone, and it had nothing to do with his damn leg.

Her wistfulness tied his stomach in knots. And her surprised response to his kiss had made his body stiff with want. That it did so despite the pain in his leg was nothing less than miraculous. He recalled when she came into his room, her hair and clothes wet and her hand dripping with blood. She'd been totally unconscious of both, worrying instead about him and, in truth, what he'd been up to.

He'd never met a woman so completely unaware of her appearance. Especially one as pretty as Sam. And she *was* pretty, even charming in a gamine way. But it was her innocence that struck him so strongly. He didn't want her hurt, and yet he didn't see any way of ending this without doing exactly that.

Thornton was a murderer, a cold-blooded killer, and Jared had no intention of letting the man's crimes go unpunished. It would go against everything he was and had been for the past ten years. He'd given the law his life and what was left of his heart. He never killed when he could avoid it. He seldom judged the men he chased, only brought them back for trial. Twice he'd proved an accused man innocent. He seldom let personal feelings interfere with duty.

But Thornton was different. He'd been Jared's crusade. The last thing he could do for his wife and sister-in-law.

Sam was just a momentary distraction. And it would be better for her if Thornton was gone. There was so much out in the world for her. He'd already noted in her an unquenchable curiosity, an interest in almost everything.

Restless, he glanced down at his book. He was three-quarters through *Les Misérables,* a novel he'd picked up in Denver. Books were good traveling companions, something to quell the loneliness of a campfire at sundown.

He picked it up. A tale of a convict's redemption and a prison guard who hounded him. It struck him as a particularly unwise choice at the moment. But Thornton wasn't wanted for stealing a piece of bread to feed a hungry family, and he—Jared—wasn't Inspector Javert, intent on hounding him for one mistake.

He put the book down.

It occurred to him—and not for the first time—that he didn't know Sam's last name. Both she and Archie had avoided mentioning it. He understood why. She could be arrested and sent to prison for shooting a U.S. Marshal. No doubt Javert would have made sure of that.

Sam might not be a killer, but Archie Smith didn't seem to have such scruples, especially if he thought Jared was a threat to her.

That he could do nothing at the moment was as agonizing as the wound. He was a restless man by nature. He'd harnessed his restlessness when he'd married Sarah, but the fact that he went to war and left her in the care of his brother was proof he hadn't completely adapted to life as a farmer.

When he'd gazed at those graves, he'd sworn he would get the murdering sons of bitches. After he'd accomplished that goal, he went after other murderers, a mission that was strengthened when Emma was killed in the stagecoach robbery.

Killed by Cal Thornton.

The search for killers, most especially Thornton, became his reason for living, the only way he could lessen the guilt he felt for not protecting his wife and child. He hadn't kept them safe, but, by God, he would protect other families, other women and children.

And that meant bringing Thornton to justice.

He closed his eyes. Tried to think of Sarah when they were first married, of her ready smile. Instead it curled up into Sam's challenging one.

He closed his eyes and pulled against the chain until it cut into his wrist. He wanted it to hurt. He wanted to be reminded he was a prisoner, not a suitor.

Remember Sarah.

She'd made it clear from the beginning what she wanted. A family to care for. A big family. From the moment he'd carried her over the threshold of the house he'd built for her, she'd tried to be the best wife in Kansas.

He tried to remember what he'd been like before the war. Before his family had been brutally murdered. He couldn't. They were two different people. He couldn't recall when he'd last really laughed. When he'd felt a moment of happiness.

Oh, he took pleasure in a sunny day, a crisp wind, or a field of wildflowers. He even took momentary physical pleasure with a woman. But actual happiness? He didn't know what the word meant any longer.

So why had he felt tugs of…bemusement whenever he engaged in a battle of wits with Samantha? Why did he look forward to each encounter when she was part of everything he'd fought against these past ten years? His heart certainly wasn't involved. It couldn't be, and yet it seemed to beat more erratically when she was with him.

He'd just been too long without a woman, he told himself.

Nothing else. Especially when she was devoted to the man who epitomized everything he hated.

SAMANTHA COULDN'T WAIT for Archie any longer.

She went back upstairs. She would get Mac into that bed, no matter what it took. Then she would go out and look for Archie and Burley. The marshal would be safe enough.

Dawg was still lying next to Mac, safeguarding him just as she'd asked.

Though Dawg was gentle with her, he could be fierce when protecting his family and his territory. He had scars from an encounter with a bear that had threatened her, and he'd almost killed a miner who'd attacked her. That was why she'd been so startled with the way he'd given his approval to the marshal. Dawg hadn't sensed danger, and he usually did.

She tried not to think of the marshal, of the amusement in his eyes as he suggested a card game, or the knowledge that she was tempted. More than tempted.

Mac was awake, trying to get up on his own. She should have known he would, and returned quicker rather than loitering with the marshal. She'd been afraid of hurting Mac even more by trying to lift him.

"Come on," she said. "I'll help. We can do it together."

He ignored her offer. "Archie isn't here?"

"No."

"What's going…on, Sam?" he asked. His gaze bored into her with the same intensity the marshal's had. "Something… sure as hell is. I know when you two are hiding something."

She couldn't lie. He knew her too well.

"Let me get you in bed first."

"No." The word was sharp and belied the paleness of his face. "I want to hear it…now."

She wanted to tell him about the marshal, but she feared he would try to go downstairs to confront the man. She reverted back to what she'd said before. "I'm just worried about that rancher."

He closed his eyes for a few seconds. "I'm not letting you

get involved in this. You and Archie leave. Find Reese. He can bring some help. I'll stay in the mine."

"I'm not leaving."

"Go," he said. "If you…give a damn about me, you'll go…."

She sat down next to him and put his good hand in hers. "You've known me most of my life. You really think I could ever be happy, knowing I left you behind?" She looked him straight in the eye. "Would you leave me?"

It was a question he didn't answer. Couldn't answer. And they both knew it.

"Come on," she said, her heart breaking to see him so helpless. "Let's get you back on the bed. The more strength you gain, the better we'll all be." He took her hand with his good one and got to his knees, then she put an arm around him and with a huge effort lifted him to the edge of the bed. He fell back on the mattress, and she lifted his feet up then sat down herself. Her breath came fast. Mac was a big man, and he was a lot weaker than the marshal.

Mac was sweaty from the exertion and his body was still too warm. Blood stained the bandage on his hand.

She'd been no more than ten minutes with the marshal but looking at Mac now, she realized she shouldn't have stayed even that long. What was it about the marshal that made her forget her responsibilities? Especially to Mac?

Mac's blue eyes were filled with pain, though she sensed it wasn't physical but the agony of not being able to protect her. "I'm going to bring you something to eat," she said. "And I'm going to sit and watch you eat every bite. We'll get out of here before anyone comes. You'll have that ranch."

"The money?" he said.

She knew he meant the funds he'd gotten for the gold. Nearly two thousand dollars. "Safe," she said. "It's in your saddlebags."

"You take it," he said. "If anyone comes, you take it and get out." He gave her a forced smile. "Promise me." His hand tightened around hers. "My life isn't worth anything if you're hurt. And one of these days, you're going to find someone…"

Her thoughts went instantly to the marshal. She rejected the idea just as quickly, couldn't even understand why it entered her head. He was without joy, without compassion, without understanding. He'd turned justice into vengeance. And yet… maybe there was a saving grace somewhere. Maybe under that lawman's badge was a heart. She meant to find it.

And she might have to kill him.

"What is it, Sam?" Mac asked.

"I…I just wish you'd married my mother."

"'Twas not for lack of wanting," he said, and a wistful look came into his eyes. "Were it not for the price on my head, I would have married her several times over. I just couldn't do that to her, and it was a mistake to keep you with me and make you a party to the constant danger."

"You never told me why," she said. "What… Why are you wanted?"

His gaze met hers and his eyes were full of regret. "You should…know who…what I was."

"I know you hired out your gun," she said.

He sighed. "I told myself the federal government owed it to me."

She didn't say anything. He'd never talked about his past. Like the marshal.

She was doing it again. Linking the two. Comparing the two.

"You know my family was killed during the war," he said slowly. "I never told you how. My father and brother were killed in battle, my sister was raped by Yankee troops and killed herself." He took a deep breath. His voice shook with emotion. "My mother moved in with another family, but died, mostly of a broken heart, I was told. I don't know. I wasn't there. I was captured and held in Elmira Prison. It was a hellhole."

He stopped for a moment as if revisiting the memories. She waited, spellbound. Mac had never told her this before, only that he'd fought in the war.

"The north claimed Andersonville was a crime, but so was Elmira. Half of us died. The other half starved and nearly perished from the cold. There was barely enough food, and the yard was nothing more than a putrid swamp that spread disease. When I finally reached home after the war, nothing was left. No family. The land had been confiscated." He looked at her. "I headed west with some friends, all of us carrying a load full of rage. War is one thing. Rape and murder another."

His voice was growing weaker. The memories were exhausting him. She wanted to hear more. She wanted an answer to her question. She wanted to hear words that would prove the marshal wrong.

It didn't matter, though. She loved Mac, regardless. She would protect him with everything in her.

He fell against the pillow. The rest of his story would have to wait.

The marshal said Mac had killed a woman. She hadn't believed it then and she didn't believe it now. She remembered how Mac had become her mother's protector after Pa died, and how he looked after the soiled doves, as well. They were all a bit in love with him, but he'd had no eyes for anyone but her mother. Even at eleven, she'd known that. He'd become a fixture in her world, disappearing from time to time on some job, but always returning with a gift for both her mother and herself. She still had most of them, including a jeweled locket he'd given her mother that had a painted miniature of Sam inside.

He closed his eyes, and she knew he was finished talking.

She studied Mac. There had never been any man-and-woman feelings between them. He was too much a father to her.

She went to the window. Still no Archie in the distance, and it was late afternoon. He should be back. Could something have happened to him? Had the hired killers overtaken him and Jake and Ike? It shouldn't happen. They could see the approaching riders from far enough away that they could come back and help get Mac to the mine.

Should she ride out to check on Archie? She was growing increasingly worried about him.

If she left again, would the marshal make more noise and alert Mac? She truly couldn't figure how the marshal could get loose, and Mac had exerted himself into exhaustion.

Maybe she should check on the marshal first. She grabbed a deck of cards from the supply they had under the bar and unlocked his doors.

He was awake, his eyes cool and guarded. The only time she hadn't seen them like that was when he talked about his wife, Sarah. She couldn't forget the pain with which each word was spoken, the grief that had frozen all other emotions. He turned toward her, and from the sudden jerk of his body, she knew the wound must still hurt like blazes. She sometimes forgot about his injured leg because he seemed to ignore it.

She put the deck on his bed beside the book. "I haven't read that one," she said, and couldn't keep a note of longing from her voice. "What is it about?"

He shrugged. "Redemption," he finally said.

Redemption. She liked that. Something in his eyes told her that wasn't the whole story. Maybe Mac had read it. She would ask him.

"Will you play that game of poker?" he asked.

"No. Solitaire will have to do now."

"I'm hungry," he said.

For some reason, she really didn't believe him. He wanted to annoy her with demands.

Still, she was tempted. She was always tempted by him. It was becoming a curse.

But worry over Archie won out. "Later," she said, then turned and left before she fell under his spell again.

11

THE RAIN SLACKENED. There was still a drizzle, but the torrents were gone. Still, the creek would be near impassable for the next few days. The trail along the bottom of the pass would be slippery, as well. It was difficult for horses to navigate the path at the best of times.

One thing she knew. Archie should have been back by now.

She should have gone instead of him. Archie could have more easily taken supplies to the cave.

Where was he?

She saddled her horse and headed out. Anything could have happened to him.

It was good to get away from the saloon, from the marshal and her compulsion to cross swords with him, and, God help her, to feel her body against his. Shivers—warm and tingling—ran through her at the remembrance. She was pulled by competing loyalties. A man she had loved like a father, and a man who was showing her how to be a woman.

She reached the trail that twisted through the pass. She didn't take it but turned onto a barely visible path that ran to the top of the pass. During the Civil War, miners kept watch up there. The gold was abundant then, and miners made weekly trips out with gold and back with supplies. There had been fears of Confederate raiders, and the camp kept sentries posted above.

Her horse stumbled once, then she saw two figures, one on a horse and one on a mule. She waited for them to reach her.

Archie's face was flushed. From the clenched expression of his mouth, she knew his legs were aching. His eyebrows lifted as she neared.

"Thought you were taking care of Mac," he said.

She moved her horse next to his as they started down the hill. "He fell. I got him up on the bed and he's all right, but I was worried about you. It was such a long time...."

"Guess I shoulda thought about that," he said. "Jake and I started talking and decided to get a small surprise ready for anyone coming up that pass. It took longer than I thought."

"Surprise?" She looked at Burley, who grinned from ear to ear.

"Boulders," he replied proudly. "We piled rocks and boulders above the pass. Me and Jake and Ike and Archie. If the marshal ain't lying and a posse comes after Mac, we'll let them rocks go and block the pass."

"Then they will know we're here."

"Could be," Archie said, "but maybe not. It's been raining for several days. Rocks and gravel are loose. If no one sees Jake or Ike, they may think it's just a natural rock slide."

"Are there enough rocks to actually block the trail?" she asked dubiously.

"Get some of them big boulders going, and they're gonna carry a hell of a lot of dirt and rock down with them. They won't be able to clear it without dynamite."

Sam thought there were a lot of *ifs* in the plan.

He saw her hesitation. "Sam, they might have a tracker with them. If so, they would find the mine pretty quick, and we'd be trapped. Even if the slide doesn't completely block the pass, it will slow them down enough that Jake and Ike can pick them off."

"I can help."

"It practically killed you to shoot that marshal fella. I ain't gonna add any more to that load."

Maybe he wouldn't, but she would. And she wasn't sure she liked the plan. They would still be confined to the valley until the stream became passable. It was clear, though, that Archie didn't relish the idea of being trapped. She didn't, either.

"I should have been here to help," she said.

"You're doing enough," he insisted. "But I don't like leaving that marshal alone. He could start hollering, and Mac would do his best to git down there."

Sam didn't think the marshal was the hollering type. He was more of a plotter. He would be lying there trying to figure a way to outsmart them.

And she had been worried about Archie. She knew Burley wouldn't be much help if they had a problem.

She averted her face from Archie. They had been together so long that he often knew what she was thinking before she thought it, even if it was something he disagreed with. He was better at it than Mac and Reese, who always saw the best in her.

How would Archie feel if he realized she was so…distracted by the marshal?

"How's the marshal?" he asked suddenly, confirming her suspicion.

"Restless," she said. "He's not a man content to do nothing, even with that leg. He…doesn't seem to mind pain."

"He minds it all right," Archie said. "He just chooses not to let his enemies see it." He eyed her. "I asked you before if he tried anything."

It was a question more than a statement.

"No," she lied. "It's just…disquieting to have him so near Mac."

She paused. "Jake's going to stay up there?" she asked, wanting to change the subject.

"Ike, too. They decided to stay together. If they see anyone coming, one of them can start the rock slide while the other warns us. Burley will take food and water up to them."

She nodded. They had a plan. With luck, they wouldn't have to use it.

JARED STARED at the cards in front of him. He'd won again, but then he was playing against himself. It was a mindless activity, something to keep him occupied. There was the book, but he seemed to have lost his taste for it.

Javet. The obsessed policeman. Damn it to hell. Jared wasn't anything like him.

Javet was a loner, too.

Jared had definitely become one. It was easier that way. No one to worry about. No one to be responsible for. No guilt to ride with him other than what was already ingrained in him.

Maybe he hadn't realized the toll it had taken on him.

Lord Almighty, but he was tired of being alone. He hadn't allowed himself to think about it before, but Sam's loyalty to the outlaw made him realize how very empty his life was. No one would give a damn if he died here in a bad-luck town.

His boss might be temporarily inconvenienced, but Jared knew he'd always been an irritant to the marshal service. He'd been told more than once that he pushed independence too far.

But the loneliness he felt now ran deep and painful. Perhaps it had been the open affection between Sam and Archie, or the obviously strong ties between the three: Sam, Archie and MacDonald. She loved with her heart and soul, and he'd felt nothing for years. Even facing Sam in the street, he had felt no fear. He'd had damn little to lose.

He gathered the cards and shuffled them. Because of the chain, he had to twist his body so he could use both hands, and that was both awkward and painful.

He wondered how much it would hurt if Sam was under him. Like hell, but it would be worth it. He told himself that all he felt was a carnal need, but he knew that wasn't true. His body wanted her—he grew hard and hot whenever she entered the room—but his heart kicked in, as well. It smiled when she did. And something jabbed him in the gut when she fastened those big, earnest eyes on him. He wanted to touch her, hold her tight. He wanted to run his fingers through the short ringlets.

He wanted to tease her and make her laugh, awaken the passion that simmered beneath her appealing innocence.

And he wanted to protect her against hurt. He swallowed hard at that.

He couldn't protect her. Not against Benson's men if they arrived, and not against himself, when he intended to destroy her world by taking away someone she loved without reservation.

He groaned inwardly. How could he compromise everything he was, everything that had meant anything these past years? The simple fact was, he couldn't. He honored his badge and, more importantly, he honored the oath he'd made beside Emma's body. Take those away, and he was nothing.

If only he could make Sam see what MacDonald was, or at least persuade her that he would be safer under Jared's control than that of paid killers. He needed to convince her that if MacDonald really cared about her, he wouldn't allow her to be placed in the line of fire.

He worried that she and the old man weren't taking Benson and his threats seriously. But he was afraid the more he pushed it, the more she would doubt him. He judged that it would take Benson another few days to hire the men he wanted, and then to track him.

How long had it been since she'd left? He couldn't tell with only the oil lamp for light. There was little difference between day and night except when the door was open. There was a watch in his saddlebags. Something else to ask for. His requests flustered her, and he found it fascinating to watch the changes in her face. She wanted him to think she was as tough as any man, but it was quite obvious that guilt hounded her for shooting him.

Where was she? Had he been left here while MacDonald made his escape? He hadn't heard any noise for hours. *It's a possibility.* It was also a possibility that they'd planned to leave him here to die. But that thought quickly passed. She would never do that.

But would Archie?

The key turned in the lock. He tensed. It was like a story he'd read. Was a lady or a tiger behind the door?

Archie walked in. Alone. He looked more tired than he had before. He was wet, and his breathing was raspy. He limped, but Jared remembered the strength in that wiry body when the old man had helped carry him inside.

"Thought I better check that leg," he said. "Also thought you might need help in tending to some other needs."

He did. Jared didn't say anything as Archie helped him with the chamber pot, then removed the bandages from his leg. Not as gently as Sam did, but expertly. "Looks clean," Archie said. "Probably don't need no more of them poultices."

"I heard a noise upstairs earlier," Jared said casually. "Sounded like someone fell."

Archie shrugged. "I knocked over a chair. My sight ain't so good these days."

It wasn't exactly what Samantha had said. Jared visually searched Archie's body. No gun or knife visible. The old man had left the key to the door out of reach, but what about the one to the handcuffs? Maybe he had it on him.

"The key to the handcuffs is upstairs," Archie said as if he'd read his mind.

Jared relaxed slightly. It had been worth a try.

"You get any ideas of escape right out of your head," Archie said. "I'm an old man and I don't mind dying. Don't mind killing, either."

Jared didn't even try to protest. Archie was no fool.

Archie looked down at the deck of cards on the bed and raised an eyebrow.

"Sam took pity on me," he said.

The old man's eyebrows rose even more at his casual use of Sam's name.

Jared cursed himself. He should have been more careful. He shrugged. "I don't know what else to call her," he explained. "Miss…what?"

The old man glowered at him.

Jared ignored it. "There's a watch in my saddlebags. Can I hope to get it back?"

Archie gave him an amused look. "I don't think so. Wouldn't want anything to happen to a handsome piece like that. Wouldn't like you to figure that one of them little parts might unlock them irons."

"Wouldn't consider it," Jared replied. "That watch was my father's."

Archie smiled. "Then you won't mind me keeping it nice and safe," he said just before he left the room, closing the door behind him.

ON THEIR ARRIVAL back at the saloon, Sam had started to go to the marshal's room.

Archie stopped her. "I think you'd better change those wet clothes. Your mama died of pneumonia. Don't want the same to happen to you. I'll check on the marshal, then Mac."

She'd nodded reluctantly while he headed for the marshal's room. She resisted the temptation to argue. It was only too obvious she wasn't to be part of whatever he wanted to discuss with their prisoner.

Another kind of chill ran through her. What if he believed there was an…attraction between her and the marshal?

"I'll meet you in Mac's room," she said, and went up the steps to her own bedroom. She stopped halfway and looked down to see Archie unlocking the door to the marshal's room and disappearing inside.

She changed her clothes, hanging her wet ones on a hook to dry. She wished she had something pretty, but that was a nonsensical notion now when everyone she loved was in danger. Archie's plan to bring down part of the mountain brought home the fact that he thought there might be truth to the marshal's claim that gunmen were on the way.

She found herself shivering.

When she finished drying her hair, she went out into the hall and met Archie. They walked to Mac's room together.

"That marshal has no right to be gittin' better so fast," he grumbled. Then he looked her in the eye. "We're going to have to tell Mac about him. Maybe not at this moment, but soon."

She nodded. He had to know. Maybe he would have some ideas about what to do.

"Woulda been better if you killed him," Archie said, not for the first time.

Sam listened while Archie scolded Mac about trying to get up and checked his wounds. He changed Mac's bandages with her help.

"You gonna have to stop doing this," he told Mac. "I'm too old to keep lookin' after you."

Mac smiled at him. "You have to keep me around. No one else could tolerate you."

"Jest remember you need to heal. No more trying to get out of that bed."

"Maybe some food would help," Mac said. "No more broth."

Immense relief flooded Sam. That was the Mac she knew. "Coming up," she said.

"I'll stay and look at his wounds," Archie said.

Maybe after preparing the food, she would have time with the marshal. Maybe she could find out more about the paid posse he'd mentioned. It could be a lie, something he'd made up to scare her into surrendering Mac.

Her heart pounded harder, then she thought of the pass and the possibility of riders. The rain made it unlikely for the next couple of days. Very few men would tackle the narrow ledges and sharp drop-offs at night or during a rainfall. Slides were notorious. But then would strangers know that?

After putting together the makings of a gooseberry pie, she plopped it in the fireplace oven, then cut what was left of the haunch of venison Ike had brought a week earlier. She had smoked it, then used some of it for the stew. Now she cut the remainder into small pieces. She planned to fry them in bacon grease, then add water and flour, along with some herbs for the gravy. She sliced potatoes and put them in another pan with salt and pepper.

Sam glanced at the door once more. How could she want so badly to open it?

Later.

While the meat and pie were cooking, she prepared dough for baking bread the next day. Anything to keep busy, to keep her mind from the man a few feet away. This might be one of the last really good meals they would have.

Before long, supper was ready and she was taking the food upstairs. Archie was entertaining Mac with one of his adventures. She never knew whether they were true or not, and Mac had probably heard them all, but he was listening.

He brightened at the sight of the steaming plates, but as he moved to sit up she saw the pain carve even deeper lines in his face.

"You look better," she said, giving him one of the plates along with a fork. "The pie's gooseberry. Your favorite."

"You sure take after your ma," Mac said. "Best cooking in the territory." The compliment never failed to please Sam. She'd learned from her mother, had helped her cook for the boarders and others who came to her table for breakfast, dinner or supper. From the time she was seven, she'd helped pour, stir and serve. "Need any water?"

"We have enough," Archie said.

She hurried downstairs and fixed a plate for the marshal. She cut his meat and included only a slice of pie. Then she unlocked the door. She took a deep breath and went inside.

He was playing with the cards. She wasn't prepared for the surprised smile. Not sardonic. Not wry. But a smile that escaped before he could take it back. It completely changed his face. And then, as if he'd caught himself, it faded.

"I brought some food," she said.

A lock of dark hair fell over his forehead and his eyes were half-open. "I've been wondering when you would feed me." He struggled to a sitting position.

She handed him the plate, and he looked at it with wry amusement. "I see the meat is already cut."

"I wanted to be of help," she said as sweetly as she could.

"You were gone for a long time." It was a question more than a statement.

"We're not your servants," she retorted.

"No," he agreed.

"I expect this is better than a jail cell."

"You're here, so yes."

He'd done it again. Disarmed her. But despite his light words, there was a glittering intensity in his eyes, a fierce indication of a powerful will.

Instead of intimidating her, though, it made her heart ache almost unbearably. She wanted him with every fiber of her being. As their gazes met, tension arced between them, filling the air with a hungering need. She knew he felt it, as well, from the muscle that leaped along a tightened jaw.

He turned his gaze from her and took a bite. Then he looked at her with a piercing gaze. "It's good," he said with a slight smile.

It was as much of a compliment as she was likely to get from him. The smile warmed her straight through to the end of her toes. If only she knew how to cope with the turmoil inside her, that hot aching need.

He seemed not to notice her confusion and eagerly ate the meat, chewing each piece with a satisfaction that was a pleasure to watch. Then he got to the pie. When he finished he slowly ran his tongue along his lips to capture every crumb. She never knew watching someone eat could be so…provocative.

It was all she could do to keep from reaching out to him, from touching those lips. Then moving her fingers to the dimple that emphasized the strength of his features rather than softening them. She wanted to explore his body with her hands and she wanted him to do the same to hers.

Her skin was on fire at the mere thought. Maybe if she hated him, she wouldn't have such feelings. But try as she might, she couldn't, not after hearing him talk so heart-wrenchingly about his wife and child. She remembered how he had charmed Dawg, and she'd seen those glimpses of humor that flashed in his eyes.

He had many sides and she liked all but one, and that one was the most important.

Almost without noticing she moved next to him, drawn like a piece of metal to a magnet. Tension sizzled between them, making a shambles of the calm she wanted to project. Her eyes searched frantically for something other than his rigid body. She took the plate from him and placed it on the floor, aware that his dark eyes were watching every movement. She reached for the deck of cards, and they went fluttering like feathers over him. She, who could handle a deck of cards like any card cheat.

His eyes were partially curtained by thick black lashes, but she saw a flame deep within. Conflicted, she reached out to gather the cards, and their hands touched. A tremor ran through his body, and her own trembled at the surge of heat between them. Her control was seeping away, lost in all those soft, needy sensations.

He pulled her to him, but unlike before there was nothing angry in the action. Instead his cheek brushed hers and stayed there for a fraction of a moment in a gesture so tender she thought her heart would crack. Then he pulled her against his chest and she heard the steady beat of his heart. It seemed to pulse through her, too. She relished the moment's closeness, the smell and feel and touch of him. The...unexpected tenderness he exuded.

Every nerve tingled. She felt bold and shy, reckless and cautious, sure and uncertain. Her heart hurt and her body ached, and a storm was building inside, fed by his touch. He shifted, using his free hand to guide her up until her cheek rested against his rough one again. She relished the heat of his body, even through their clothes. New sensations spiraled through her, each one more powerful than the next.

She closed her eyes, the better to feel. And feel she did. For the first time, she felt truly alive. As if she'd just been drifting along until now, waiting, only she hadn't known it.

His lips touched hers. Not like the last time, with anger and need, but lazily. Lips touching lips with gentle exploration, each brush prolonging a magical moment. She put her hands around his neck and played with the muscles there.

She opened her eyes to see the dark blue of his. Usually so curtained, so careful, they were anything but. They were scorching. Intense. And suddenly...sad.

He touched her face with a gentleness she hadn't expected. She sensed the restraint in him...felt it in the tenseness of his body. She didn't want restraint. She wanted to pursue all these feelings to wherever they led.

"You should go," he said lightly, as if to disperse the weighty emotions settling around them.

She knew he was right. He was still her enemy and she was his captor, and their goals were diametrically opposed. But she couldn't. Her skin was alive with feeling, with wanting, and the core of her was a mass of writhing nerve ends. She had to take this ride to the moon.

"No," she protested.

With a groan, he released her and guided her body to the side of the bed. When she looked at him she saw agony in his eyes, and she knew it wasn't altogether from his leg.

He touched her cheek. "I have no right," he said.

"I'm giving you that right," she murmured.

"Nothing has changed," he said softly. "Nothing at all."

But it had. To her, it had.

Except for Mac. The marshal was right. *That* was the same.

She stiffened. "You won't change your mind about Mac?"

"Is that what you thought?" he said, his tone suddenly harsh. "A kiss would make me forget I'm a marshal?"

Tears pricked her eyes, but she wasn't going to let him see them. For a moment she had forgotten everything but the feel and touch of him. She was angry now, but it was mostly at herself.

"Of course not," she said. "How could I ever be so foolish as to forget that?"

Her heart pounded. Had she really misled herself into thinking he was attracted to her? That he cared about anything beyond getting free? Getting free and hanging Mac?

Her heart pounded and she felt sick to her stomach. Well, she could play the same game.

She sat up, then stood. She ran a finger through her curls and tried to get some part of her sanity back. The cards were all over the bed and floor. Some were bent. She decided to leave them there. Her legs were unsteady, and her body still hummed from his touch, but she didn't want him to know that. Better he think that she'd kissed him only for Mac's sake. Not her own.

For Mac.

The posse. Ask him about the posse. Then leave with dignity.

"You haven't said anything more about the posse you mentioned."

His eyes were suddenly alert. "Then you believe me?"

"I might," she said. "But why do you think they could find this valley?"

"They could figure it out like I did. Start where the men were shot. Keep going in the direction Thornton was headed. I'd heard years ago that he was holed up in some mining town, but I never knew which one. This time I asked the right questions and came up with Gideon's Hope. It suddenly seemed logical."

"Maybe they're not as...persistent."

"With the kind of money being offered, some of those gun hands would go to the ends of the earth."

She made the mistake of looking into his eyes. She saw worry, and something close to understanding. "He will be better off with me," he continued. "And so would you."

She almost lost herself in those eyes. She almost believed him, but she also knew no court would give Mac a chance. "No," she said sharply as she tried to ignore the intense craving in her belly.

Her back stiff, she left the room and locked the door before she did or said something she would regret.

12

LETTING HER GO had been one of the hardest things Jared had ever done. Letting her believe that all he wanted was MacDonald was another.

He couldn't remember when he'd wanted a woman so badly. The fact that she'd been not only willing but eager made his words that much more difficult.

He ached all over. The pain in his leg had exploded when her leg had touched it. But then other parts of his anatomy were on fire, as well. He hadn't expected that, at least not to this extent. There was a connection—a sexual tension—between them that he'd never felt before. But he'd thought he could control it.

She'd felt so perfect in his arms. So right. Her face had been so incredibly wistful and enchanting in the glow of the oil lamp. He saw her lips again in his mind's eye. Trembling and stretched into a shy, tentative smile that reached into his heart and squeezed so hard he could barely breathe.

While he had hoped to persuade her, he also knew she'd had the same motive. But somehow both had become lost in the overwhelming passion that had swept over both of them.

A groan escaped his lips. How had he allowed this to go so far? He didn't like seeing himself as a despoiler.

When had his job become so important he was ready to discard every scruple he had?

He started picking up the scattered cards. He couldn't reach them all, but he stacked the ones he could and placed them on the chair near the bed. The others would have to wait.

He found himself smiling as he remembered the chagrined look on her face when the deck virtually exploded from her hand. She was probably a good poker player. There seemed to be no end to her talents. Nothing seemed to frighten her.

She was a walking mass of contradictions, of toughness and unconscious femininity. When he put them all together, he had to admit someone had done well in raising her. Except for the fact she had shot him—which was a big *except*—she was smart and kind and competent. Her joy for life was evident, and she had a heart that loved well, too well.

Damn, what a mess he'd made.

She'd left the oil lamp on low, too low to read. It was out of his reach, and he couldn't turn it up. He was left with pain and memories and self-disgust to pass the time, and none were satisfactory.

He turned on his side.

He suspected it was going to be a long, lonely night. And he was worried. He couldn't get that posse out of his mind. They wouldn't care if Sam was in the cross fire, and he knew her well enough now to realize she would be in the middle of things.

But why would MacDonald allow her to stay if he thought she was in danger? That question bothered Jared. And why hadn't the outlaw been in to see him if he was in the valley? And if he wasn't, why was Sam so worried about the posse?

One idea kept pounding at him, though, and it wouldn't go away. How could someone like Sam love and respect the man Jared wanted? Love him enough to risk her life. Love him enough to shoot another human being.

Women had been known to love bad men. But she loved this man like a father. Sam was no one's fool. She would recognize evil, even in a father figure, and he didn't think she would condone it.

He wondered now whether he was chasing the right man.

SAM WASHED all the pots and pans and dishes. From now on they would be eating mostly bacon and beans. There was still half a pie, and bread dough was rising. She would bake it at first light. But the last of the venison was gone.

Everything else was ready. Half their supplies were in the cave. The other half were in bundles in the saloon. She had little to do, and that annoyed her. She needed to keep busy. She needed to divert her mind from the man just feet away from her.

Rain slashed against the windows, and a clap of thunder rocked the building. Her first instinct was a prayer of thanks. More rain would further delay any posse. Maybe long enough for Mac to heal. Maybe enough to raft down the stream.

She also thought how miserable both Ike and Jake must be, up watching the pass.

Sam filled pitchers of water. She would take one to Mac and Archie, although she expected both would be asleep. The marshal already had plenty of water. She put several logs in the fireplace and poured water into a pot to heat. She would use that to wash.

Then she sat and waited for it. She was restless, thinking about her time with the marshal. She'd been wanton. Maybe too wanton. Her face flushed as she remembered his rejection.

She looked down at her britches and shirt. Was that it? The fact she didn't look like a woman.

Another roll of thunder roared through the building, this one louder than before. It would have woken the marshal if he slept. Possibly Mac, too. She took the water upstairs to Mac's room. Both he and Archie were asleep.

Dawg raised his head, then got up lazily and followed her out. She stopped by her room, picked up her guitar and took it downstairs. She sat in one of the chairs by the window and watched the storm with Dawg beside her. Despite his presence, loneliness echoed in her.

She strummed the notes to a song. A lullaby. Then her fingers went to "Lorena." Lightning streaked through the sky, revealing the muddy road, the dilapidated building on the other side of it. Bombarded by emotions, she feasted on a sight most would probably consider sad. Not her. This had been her home since she could remember. Her mother's and father's graves were a block away in the haphazard cemetery. She had been a child in this place, and still felt only half-grown, too inexperienced to know the ways of men and women.

She blinked back tears. She cared about the marshal. Too much. Maybe she even loved him. And she didn't know what to do about it. She had hoped to convince him that Mac was not the man he thought him to be. She wanted the marshal to trust her. But then maybe he wanted her to trust him.

She felt as if she were betraying Mac. And yet she couldn't stop thinking about the marshal and that half smile and those intense dark blue eyes and the strong body that was a thing of beauty.

Dawg nudged her as though he knew something was very wrong. She shook herself back to reality. The water should be ready.

She left the guitar on the chair. The boiling water, when mixed with water from the pump, would be enough to wash herself, if not to make a bath.

She turned off all but one oil lamp and went upstairs. She refused to look at the marshal's room. No more excuses to go inside. She'd used them all up.

Sam washed quickly and then looked at herself in the mirror. She frowned as she stared at her short hair and faded shirt and old britches. Plain, she thought again.

Opening her door, she looked out. She waited a few moments, grabbed her lamp by the handle and went up the narrow steps to the attic. The door was locked but she'd once watched Mac put the key on the ledge above.

Once inside, she made her way through old beds and chairs and other odds and ends. She finally found the trunk and opened it. Most of the dresses were designed to show legs and breasts. A little too red. A little too gaudy.

She needed something more subtle. She kept searching. Maybe there was another trunk. She finally found one pushed into the corner. She rifled through it. Three dresses. Two plain and one of a better quality. Nothing fancy, but the material was a pretty sky-blue, and slightly yellowed lace trimmed the neckline.

She suddenly realized she'd seen it before. Her mother had worn it the last night before she got sick. A dancing dress, she'd said. Sam held it tight for a moment, trying to find some trace of her mother in it, some comfort.

How she wished…

Sam swallowed hard, then combed through the rest of the trunk's contents. Undergarments. A night shift. Ribbons and a locket.

She hesitated, then took the blue dress. She added the locket to the pile. The dress probably wouldn't fit, and it was musty. And she had no shoes to go with it, only boots. Still she carried it down to her room, Dawg matching her steps.

To her surprise, the dress fit. Not perfectly but well enough. She gazed at a different Sam in the mirror. She had no paints. Nothing to ripen her lips or make her skin less brown from the sun. And her hair? What she wouldn't give at the moment for long golden locks.

She took off the dress and very carefully hung it in the wardrobe to air.

Tomorrow. Tomorrow she might wear it.

For tonight, she would try to get some sleep while they were safe.

If only she could stop thinking of the man below…

JARED WOKE and wondered what time it was. He'd stayed awake for hours. Thunder seemed to rumble through the room, and he could hear the rain. But what kept him awake had nothing to do with the elements, and everything to do with a bewitching sprite named Sam.

He couldn't forget the look on her face when he'd stopped what was a certain disaster for both of them.

God help him, but it had taken every bit of his willpower to stop. He'd thought, hoped even, that she would return last night. But she hadn't. She had looked confused and hurt when she'd left. He'd wounded her, and there was nothing he could do to repair the situation. He had led her on, had stimulated and aroused her with his hand and lips for his own twisted motives.

Who was he to condemn a man he didn't even know?

Javet. Inspector Javet. The damn policeman was haunting him now.

He tried to sleep, but he was too edgy. He was confounded by the sexual attraction between Sam and him, the way the air became electrified when they were together, the way their eyes locked when he had no intention of letting it happen.

Life with Sarah had been simple and comfortable and natural. Like an evening sunset. Sam, on the other hand, was all fire and storm, and he suspected she would be more challenging and exciting than...comfortable.

What in the hell am I thinking?

No doubt *she* was thinking of ways to manipulate him, to keep him from finding MacDonald. He suddenly realized he was beginning to think of Thornton as MacDonald. Resident saint.

It was obvious Thornton lived here occasionally. But how occasionally? And why hadn't Jared heard of this town during his hunt for the man now called MacDonald?

Maybe because for all practical purposes Gideon's Hope really was a ghost town and, worse, a "bad-luck town," as Sam had called it. Miners were a superstitious bunch.

The locals might also be loyal to MacDonald, keeping their knowledge of him to themselves, which was remarkable. He didn't know many outlaws who could claim that. In his experience, they usually turned against one another.

He reached over and found the pitcher. He poured himself a cup of water and drank it. Morning yet? Usually his mental clock gave him a good estimate of time, but now it was confused.

Jared yanked the chain even though he couldn't free himself. Still, the pain helped dull the frustration in his head. At least he still heard the rain. That would slow Benson's posse. But for how long?

He turned awkwardly, attacking the pillow. Maybe he could bargain with the laconic Archie. If he could face MacDonald...

He lay back and willed himself to be patient, to try to sleep. He started counting fence posts.

SAM WOKE UP with the daylight. She wasn't sure when she actually went to sleep, but her eyes felt heavy, maybe because of the tears she'd shed. She stood and looked out the window. It was still raining but more gently now. The clouds weren't as heavy and glowering.

She thought of the dress in the wardrobe, then pulled on her britches and shirt. She wasn't going to try to be something she wasn't for a man who didn't give a fig for her.

She went downstairs, Dawg padding along beside her. Archie was already up, waiting for the coffee to boil.

"You should have wakened me," she said.

"No reason. Mac's better this morning, and it's time you got more rest."

Archie seemed restless. They all were with this threat hanging over them.

He looked at the guitar she'd left on the table. "Been playing some?" She nodded.

"I've missed it," he said. "You and Reese playing together, and Mac singing."

She was surprised. Archie wasn't usually sentimental. "I'll play for you later."

He nodded. "Mac would like that. Not much else to be done today except maybe gathering all the guns together and loading 'em. Doesn't hurt to be prepared." He poured coffee into three cups. "I'll take one in to the marshal."

She felt a moment's relief. She wouldn't have to face him for a while. Wouldn't have to hide emotions that threatened to betray her true feelings.

While Archie tended to the marshal, she put the bread that

had risen into the stove, then set the beans on to boil and mixed and rolled out some biscuits. She would add bacon to the beans later. Nothing to do until then.

Why was Archie taking so long? What were they taking about?

She was fidgety, uncommonly so. She took the guitar and picked out an old folk tune. The music usually calmed her but her stomach was roiling and her fingers were clumsy.

Then the door opened again.

She continued to play as Archie locked the door and walked over to the stove. He sniffed. "Biscuits?"

Her fingers stopped plucking. "Yes."

"I'll be up with Mac," he said. "I checked the marshal's wound. It seems to have opened some. You'll need to cut another sheet for bandages."

She knew exactly how the wound had opened. She didn't want to bandage it. She didn't want to get that close to him again. But she nodded. Obviously, Archie had not sensed any… problem. Good. She nodded.

"We'll go through the saloon, then, and gather the guns and ammunition. We'll see what we've got. Include the marshal's pistol and rifle."

He took two cups of coffee and limped up the stairs. The rain was making his rheumatism worse, and that was why he'd asked her to look after the marshal again. He knew she was safe as long as he had the key to the handcuffs. He didn't know there was another kind of danger he couldn't protect her from.

She finished with breakfast preparations and went upstairs. Mac was sitting in a chair drinking coffee. He looked pale. "Archie said you had your guitar out."

She nodded. "I'll come up later and play for you."

He looked at her with searching eyes. "You look different," he said. "Even prettier. And sad."

"I've been worried about you," she replied.

"No need. I have nine lives."

"And you've used up eight and a half," she retorted. She wondered why Archie hadn't told him about the marshal yet.

Probably because he knew Mac would try to go downstairs—and agree to go with the marshal to save Sam.

She glanced over at Archie and knew she was right. She saw it in his eyes. He wanted to find some way to get rid of the marshal before Mac found out.

Her blood ran cold. Archie was not a cruel man. Despite his rough exterior he was a healer at heart. But he was also extremely loyal and would not hesitate to give up his life for a friend. Or take one.

She forced a smile and hugged Mac, then returned to the kitchen. Oddly enough, Dawg stayed with her instead of returning to Mac's side. It was as if he sensed who needed him most. She cut one of the last three worn sheets they had. At least it was clean. She put on some water to heat. Then she filled a plate with food and unlocked the door.

Apparently Archie had turned the oil lamp higher. The marshal was sitting up reading. His eyes were shadowed when he looked up at her. "Was that you playing the guitar?" he asked.

She nodded. He wouldn't have been able to hear through the door last night. It was too thick. He must have heard her when Archie left his room earlier.

"Will you play for me?"

"Maybe. In return for something else."

She put the plate on the table and the bandage on the bed, then sat down in the chair. Archie had taken off the old bandage and she saw fresh blood seeping from the wound. The burn had turned yellowish and needed cleaning, as well.

"Do you want to eat first?" she asked in the most normal voice she could manage.

His eyes didn't change. "No." Then he raised his free hand and tipped her chin to meet his gaze. "It's not your fault," he added.

It was unnerving that he seemed to read her every thought. She went back to the kitchen area for the hot water and poured some into a basin. When she returned, she concentrated totally on the wound. Washing away the fresh blood, cleaning the pus from the burn. It still looked ugly and she knew it must hurt like the very furies.

She went back to the kitchen for salve and lightly rubbed a layer over the wound, then bandaged it. When she finished, she handed him the plate of food, put his coffee on the chair where he could reach it, then left.

HUNGRY, JARED ATE QUICKLY and wondered whether she would return. He missed her every moment she was gone.

As he finished the last of his plate, Sam appeared with the guitar. Dawg was at her side and he came over and put a paw on the bed.

Jared rubbed the dog's ears and Dawg growled with pleasure, his tail waving back and forth.

She strummed a few chords, then stopped. "In return for information," she reminded him.

It was as if last night had never happened, or else she was very good at pretending. "What do you want to know?" he asked.

"Why you became a marshal, for one."

He mulled over the question. It seemed harmless enough except it was a place he didn't want to revisit, a decision that had come from bottomless pain and rage. The rage had cooled, but the grief was always there. He suspected she sensed that from what little he had already told her. He knew what she really wanted. Mercy for a killer, and that was one thing he would not grant.

He shrugged, wondering whether he was making another mistake. But he was losing himself in those damn eyes. So many different colors. Amber and gold and a little moss-green when the light from the lantern hit them just right. They seemed to change with her every mood. And he'd been struck by the music he'd heard when Archie opened the door. Still another side of her. She would always be a surprise. A challenge.

Now those eyes were steady on him. Demanding answers. And he suddenly wanted to explain. "I went after the men who killed my family. It took better than a year and…then there was nothing left for me in Kansas. I was offered a marshal's badge by someone I met along the way. Seemed as good a way as any to make a living."

She strummed the guitar. "Anything you particularly like to hear?"

He shook his head.

She started to play "Aura Lee."

He knew the song, and the haunting melody. She was good, and he wondered who had taught her to play.

When she finished, he asked, "Do you sing, too?"

She shook her head. "Not very well."

"How did you learn to play?"

"A question for a question?" she asked, wanting more information.

He nodded.

"During the mining days, the saloon employed singers… and other ladies. After my mother died, they kinda mothered me, or tried to. They taught me to play, even some lyrics." Her eyes suddenly danced. "I know some interesting ones."

She was enchanting again and his heart thumped against his chest.

"Now I get to ask a question," she said, and the sparkle was gone, replaced by deadly seriousness.

"Who was it Mac supposedly killed?" she asked without pause.

"A woman named Emma Wentworth," he said.

"You knew her? Is that why you want Mac so much?"

Jared reminded himself again not to underestimate her. He hesitated. It was personal. Real personal. Still, she should know who she was protecting. "She was my wife's sister. My sister-in-law. She was traveling to Denver. The stagecoach she was riding was held up. One of the bandits manhandled her. She protested and was shot."

"It wasn't Mac," she said, with absolute assurance.

"A member of his outlaw band said it was."

"Mac doesn't manhandle women. Ever." After a moment, she asked, "When did this happen?"

"Years ago."

"How many years?"

"That's too many questions."

"Is it? Don't you want to know what really happened?"

"I know what happened."

"Judge and jury and prosecutor, all wrapped up in one. How nice to be so infallible."

Her face had turned hard as stone. Whatever light had been there was gone now.

"He killed others, as well," he said, "and stole one hell of a lot of money from the army."

His gaze met hers and held, and he didn't want to let it go. He ached to touch her, to pull her to him and feel her softness again, to satisfy the need now settling permanently inside him. Frustration gnawed at his gut.

The air was fraught with tension again. God, how he wanted her. It was astounding to him, especially considering the injury to his leg, and who and what they both were. Prisoner and captor. Lawman and outlaw.

God help him if he didn't want to hold her again.

"I answered your question," he said. "Another song?"

She smiled sweetly and played "The Yellow Rose of Texas."

To annoy him, he knew. She was only too aware he'd served with the Union, and the song was a favorite rebel tune.

He worked at keeping a smile from his face as she finished.

"Truce?" he asked. He reached out a hand to her and watched her emotions battle each other. The silence stretched tautly between them, and suddenly nothing mattered except the need building between them.

She unconsciously licked her lips. The ache in his groin grew acute. She probably had no idea how arousing that simple act of wetting her lips was. He wondered whether she could see the swelling under the sheet.

He held out his hand. "Move closer," he whispered. He heard the intake of her breath. Then, to his surprise, she did as he asked. She looked dazed, Yet at the same time her eyes were so damned bright and curious and even...glowing. His lips descended on hers, and she responded with an eagerness that inflamed him. He deepened the kiss, almost harshly at first as if to chase her away. But her fingers went around his neck, caressing him, with so much gentleness it hurt.

Her body quivered ever so slightly. He silently cursed the chain that made every movement damned awkward. His left arm wrapped around her, drew her to him. Her body pressed against his, her cheek against the bare skin of his chest. Surprisingly, her arms went around him, gingerly at first. He felt her stiffening awareness as his arousal pressed into her.

A low moan rumbled through his body as his lips gentled against hers. His gaze met hers, and he was almost lost in the smoldering fire of that golden amber even as he sensed her uncertainty.

She was a virgin. He hesitated. Hell, she'd nearly killed him, and yet he felt a tenderness he hadn't known in a very long time.

Her mouth opened hesitantly under his lips with an unexpected longing that awakened long-dead feelings in him. His mouth hardened against hers. He forced anger because he didn't know how to deal with the tenderness. She was stirring things best left alone, and he knew he couldn't trust her.

He started to draw away, but she stopped him. She wrapped her fingers around his neck, playing with the muscles there, and his lust reached monumental proportions as heat surged to his loins.

Damn, he wanted her. His head bent and his lips touched the fine taffy-colored curls. It felt good, those curls. Soft and inviting. And then their lips met again and he knew nothing could stop the raging fire.

13

EXPLOSION!

Sam felt as if every emotion was running amok, and, worse, her body was doing the same. New sensations were bursting inside her. His lips against hers, her face against his rough one, his hand playing with the nape of her neck. Each intimacy ignited blazes throughout her entire being. And strongest of all was the irresistible craving deep in her core.

He unbuttoned the top of her shirt with his free hand. Her breast came alive with his touch, hardening and sparking fresh frissons of need coursing through her.

The embers of the fire that had glowed between them since the first day grew into an inferno. It felt painful in deliciously exquisite ways that aroused and burned her. Sam lost herself in his touch, in the taste of his lips. She didn't understand what was happening to her, why nothing mattered right now but the lawman she should fear. Her heart was racing, and her senses were spinning out of control.

He released a long breath. His hand left her breast and he held her chin in his fingers, forcing her gaze to meet his. "Not wise, Miss Sam," he said.

"No," she agreed. "Marshal." The last was her feeble attempt at sanity.

"Jared," he said. "Say it. Say Jared." His voice was low but there was a cajoling persistence.

"Jared." She tried it out, rolled it on her tongue. It was silly that the mere voicing of a name made a change, but it did. It broke down a door standing between them, a door she'd tried to barricade.

Her fingers were still on his neck and his warmth flowed through her. Their gazes locked together, and she was almost motionless, her whole being waiting for something. Waiting…

His gaze was intense, and there was a brilliant glitter in those dark hawklike eyes. His hand still held her chin and his fingers moved sensuously along her lips. She felt every one of those touches clear through to the bone and trembled, unable to control the need inside.

And what were her eyes telling *him?* She prayed the lust wasn't too obvious. Now she knew exactly what the word meant. How strong it was. How compelling. She wouldn't believe that what she felt was anything more than lust. She *couldn't.*

Pull away! And yet how could she? She'd always been an explorer, and this was the ultimate exploration.

He slid his fingers to her hair, playing with the short curls, stroking her neck with a tenderness she hadn't felt in him before. She hadn't thought of him as gentle or tender or…

She closed her eyes, savored the awareness as the very new thing it was, even though she knew she should run as if all the demons in hell were chasing her.

But she wanted more. So much more.

His lips touched hers again, tentatively this time, as if he, too, was lost in some enchanted but dangerous maze. His other kiss had been explosive. Angry. Wanting. It had lit fires deep inside, but the tentativeness of this kiss was far more treacherous. A part of her melted inside, and she tumbled into a flood of mindless sensation. As if he sensed something had changed, his tongue entered her mouth, exploring, seducing, inviting her into a world she'd never known before.

"Lie next to me," he whispered. "This is too damn awkward."

He'd pulled her shoulders and head down, but her hip was

still on the edge of the bed. She'd been careful to avoid his wound, but oh, how she wanted to feel all of him next to her.

"Your leg?"

"Damn my leg," he said as his free hand guided her down next to him on the edge of the bed. She trembled with expectancy.

He trailed his mouth to the side of her neck and nuzzled the skin, then moved upward. Heat licked at her and she put her arms around him, played with the dark hair even though she knew it was a terrible mistake. *He's the enemy,* she frantically reminded herself. But the warning was chaff in the wind, unsubstantial compared to the power of her other feelings. She wanted to prolong the dizzying, warm excitement she knew he shared, for he was rigid with need. She savored her ability to do that to him. He'd so often seemed immune to any feelings, as if nothing really touched him.

She'd always been passionate in her beliefs, in her fierce loyalties, in her love of nature and the orphaned and hurt critters that inhabited her world, but she'd sometimes wondered whether she had the type of passion she'd read about in books. Now she knew it had been lying dormant, waiting for the right man.

But this wasn't the right man, part of her screamed. This was the worst possible man.

She didn't care.

She only knew her body was reacting completely on its own, and her blood was hot, rushing like a storm-swollen river through her body.

From the moment his lips touched hers, she was helpless to resist, helpless to keep from wanting him. The knowledge was excruciating because it was a betrayal of those she loved. And yet…she was drowning in the essence of him.

Their lips met again and she stretched against him, feeling the growing hardness of his maleness. She whimpered as the pressure inside her grew. Her hand went to the back of his neck and touched and teased as he had done with her. She knew now how much that simple touch could excite and arouse.

He positioned his lips over hers, and her mouth readily opened to his.

Thunder clapped outside. It should have brought back her reason, but instead it only added to the pulsating sensations building within her. Just as she had since she'd watched him approach her in the deserted street, she warred with herself, mind against heart, body against soul.

Her tongue became every bit as aggressive as his, exploring and teasing. Her gaze met his and his eyes were no longer that cool, impenetrable darkness, but alive and blazing, the blue in them more obvious than ever.

She pulled back for a moment, seeking a respite from the emotions that were overruling every sensible, responsible part of her. She felt a bewildering pain in her heart, a longing for something she didn't understand, and the strength of it terrified her.

WHAT HAD STARTED as a game, a challenge, had suddenly become something else. Jared's lips took hers. Hard. Part of him wanted to scare her away. The other...hell, the other wanted her with a need he'd never felt before.

God, but she was beautiful. And soft. So damned soft.

And so damned innocent. It was obvious with her every response. This was all new to her.

Damn MacDonald for keeping her here. She should have been courted, married, with child. Yet he was grateful, as well. In just a few days, she'd awakened a heart he'd long thought dead. He'd felt alive and even eager for the next time he would see her. Hell, he'd felt like a callow kid courting his first girl. Nothing could have surprised him more.

Then her lips reached for his and her body stretched against his, and all thought evaporated as their lips played and teased and tasted. Dammit, he burned with need for her. He burned so much that the pain in his leg disappeared. His need reached volcanic proportions as she touched his neck and returned his kiss with such surprised...wonder.

Had she even been kissed before?

He doubted it now. Dammit, she embraced everything she did with all that was in her. She was even willing to kill and be killed for a friend or whatever it was that MacDonald/Thornton was to her. How could he turn that against her now and live with himself?

He closed his eyes and held her tight with his free arm, wanting, needing desperately to plunge into her, but then he would be no better than the men he'd chased. He would be killing something in her....

"Don't stop," she said, her voice soft but determined.

"What about MacDonald?" he said roughly.

She was silent.

"I'm still going after him."

"I know."

Her voice was little more than a whisper, and there was pain in it. Maybe like the pain in his gut. But he could no more change who he was than she could.

Her lips moved closer to him, and this time she was the aggressor. Innocent or not, she wanted him as much as he wanted her. He touched her face with his fingers, wondering how he'd ever thought, even for a second, that she was anything but female. She was lightly tanned and he could see a few freckles on her nose, but the skin was flawless. Her eyes were enormous now, the colors constantly changing. He could drown in those eyes.

He could drown in her.

He couldn't help but touch the fine lines of her face, trace his fingers along her cheek. He hated being restrained, unable to take her in both arms and bring her even closer to him. But with every movement, he was reminded of the chain holding him, and the division between them, and the folly of what he was doing.

Her lips curled in a smile that was all feminine and seductive and yet uncommonly endearing at the same time. She had to be in her twenties, but she was an intoxicating combination of hellion and angel.

She took his hand and played with it for a moment, then she

moved closer and their lips touched again. No punishment this time. No anger. Just an exploration that started tentatively, then grew bolder.

"Sam," he said. "Samantha." At the moment, the latter name fit her better.

He couldn't hold her, or lift himself above her. He couldn't do what he wanted to do. Seduce her. That had been his idea several days ago, but now the thought repelled him. He wanted to make love to her. Slowly, with care.

The pressure inside grew, and he felt ready to explode. Her hand touched his thigh. He guided it to his penis. Watched and felt—God, how he felt—as she touched him. And then to his surprise she was taking off her clothes, letting them slide to the floor. She looked both defiant and determined.

"Are you sure?" he asked.

She nodded.

"You could have a child," he warned. "We could," he amended.

She looked offended. "I know that."

"You're beautiful," he said. And she was. She was slender with just enough curves to give her a satisfying softness. He held out his hand and she lay next to him as the heat between them blazed. She touched his chest, lingered on a scar, then ran her fingertips downward, along the skin that stretched taut over the ridged muscles of his abdomen. He shuddered, trying to prevent the spasms her touch created. Yet all his fabled control was crumbling, pulled down by a woman who was part imp and part siren.

His free hand went to the soft mound between her legs. She gasped with surprise, then cried out in startled pleasure as her body arched toward him. He twisted himself—damn the chain—to meet her and felt the heat run like lightning between them, scorching and branding.

TREMORS SHUDDERED THROUGH Sam as his lips touched hers, and he moved his fingers first to one of her breasts and then lower to her most private place. Sizzling fires danced up and down her spine.

"Are you sure you want to be here?" he whispered in her ear.

No, Sam wasn't sure. She wasn't sure of anything, but that didn't diminish the need in her.

"Yes," she said instead.

She heard the rattle of the chain as he strained against it, and for a second the magic was broken.

She drew a shaky breath, trying to restore some calm to a body possessed by a storm. He trailed his lips down her cheek and to her ear, nuzzling until she knew nothing but a consuming need for him, and she couldn't break away now if her life depended on it. His tongue feathered her cheek even as his fingers continued to explore the place no man had touched before. Sensations streaked through her, and she whimpered with the fierce desire clawing at her.

"Samantha," he whispered.

Her name sounded fine on his lips. Different. But she didn't have time to think because he engaged her mouth again, and she touched his chest. Hard. So hard. She fingered one of the scars and looked up at him. He would have another scar because of her. She swallowed hard. "Your leg?" she said. "I don't want…"

He dismissed her words. "I've ridden for days with worse wounds."

His lips chased the guilt away, and she ran her hands down his body while he continued to tease and arouse, sending shimmering waves of heat through every part of her until she couldn't bear more.

"Jared." It was a cry of pure need.

She was aware he moved as far as his chained wrist would allow. He balanced himself over her, and she thought briefly of the wound, the stress…

And then he lowered himself, most of his weight on his good leg. She felt the throbbing of his sex against her and the aching craving became even stronger. She cried out again as he entered her. Pain came so quickly she couldn't contain a small gasp.

He hesitated.

"Don't stop," she said. Despite the pain, the raw need was building inside her. He moved again, fitting himself slowly to her, and the pain started to fade, replaced by waves of delicious sensations as he penetrated deeper and deeper, as if searching for the core of her soul. Her body instinctively moved with his as his rhythm quickened and waves of ecstasy rolled through her. And then when she thought she could bear no more, she felt a magnificent explosion inside. Thunderous waves of pleasure swept through her like a great tidal wave....

14

JARED SUDDENLY WITHDREW from her but held her close as she felt moisture between her legs. She knew why, and she also realized what it had just cost him. He lay beside her, his heart beating rapidly, a muscle throbbing in his cheek.

She touched his lips with her fingers as he rolled over on his side. Her body was still alive with the aftershocks, frissons of pleasure running through her.

"Is it always like this?" she asked.

"No," he said. "Hardly ever...like this."

She put her head on his chest. It was damp with sweat and she was intoxicated with the scent of him.

His free arm went around her. She wished she had the key to the handcuffs so she could be engulfed in his arms. It seemed that Archie had been wise to keep it.

She couldn't decide whether she could trust Jared. Even now when she had given herself to him both with her body and her heart, she couldn't be sure. That hurt to the core.

She didn't want to think of that. She just wanted to revel in all the new sensations that still rocked her body. *Sated*. That was the word.

Another Reese word she had never understood fully until now.

She turned, careful of his leg, and ran her fingers along his chest and up over the ridges of his hard face, the sun lines and the dark eyebrows that could glower so well.

She'd never known there could be such simple joy in touching.

He closed his eyes even as fingers kneaded the back of her neck. She put her head against his heart and heard it beat. She knew she should leave. Archie might well kill him if he caught them together, even if it was her fault.

"Samantha," he finally said. "I like the sound of your name."

"I like the way you say it."

"This is a damn fool thing to do," he said.

He tugged at the chain absently.

She met his gaze directly. "I don't have the key."

"Archie is a wise man," he said.

Would he have used these minutes to free himself and go after Mac? Was he only using her now?

A chill ran through her. She'd thought...believed...he was as caught up with the fire between them as she was.

As if he knew exactly what she was thinking, he touched her face with a tenderness that was unexpectedly painful. It was accompanied by something else she couldn't quite define. Regret? Maybe uncertainty? It was so hard to tell with him.

Yet she couldn't stop herself from touching him. She was sore where he'd been, and yet a craving for him was still curling inside her. She'd just started exploring an entirely new world and she didn't want to stop now. Her fingers moved along the muscles of his stomach, and she felt them tightening.

"Don't begin something I can't stop," he warned, but there was a hint of a smile on his lips.

She leaned over and kissed him, slowly, and felt the fires beginning again. "I think I like starting 'somethings.'"

His gaze caught hers, held it. "Does anything ever scare you?"

"You do," she said. "I want you, and I know I shouldn't. I think you want me, too, but I don't know how much. I don't know if you bed every woman you meet, and I don't know whether I should care. I..." She swallowed hard. "I thought...I could just..."

"Use me?" he said wryly.

"Not exactly," she said. "I wanted..." She was tripping over her words. She couldn't say what she felt. She couldn't give him that advantage.

"And now you know," he said, his voice suddenly hard and his eyes cold. "I think you had better go, Miss Sam. It wouldn't do for your Archie to find you here in the enemy's arms."

She didn't want to leave. She didn't want to stop touching him. But he had suddenly distanced himself. She'd made a mess of trying to explain herself, but she was too confused by the wash of new emotions to know exactly what she felt.

Enemy. He thought she was using him.

But wasn't she doing exactly that?

She stood. Looked down at him in the flickering light of the lantern on the table. His eyes met hers steadily, and the deep blue she sometimes saw was eclipsed in their blackness. He looked dangerous and angry and suddenly untouchable.

She pulled on her now wrinkled clothes and started for the door.

"You might want to get clean sheets," he said in a cool, dispassionate voice.

She suddenly became aware of the scent lingering in the room and the stains on the sheets. Her face flared, but she knew he was right. Archie would be checking his leg in the morning.

Without answering him, she opened the door and closed it behind her. She took a deep breath. Her body still sang from his touch. From their lovemaking. Ripples of sensation reminded her of the pleasure that so recently rocked her body. But just as strong was the memory of the way his eyes had shuttered and his face hardened. Just as strong was the pain. He had felt nothing. Or at least, very little. His face had told her that.

A tear slid down her cheek. One lone tear. Then another.

She angrily wiped it away. She never cried. *Never.* At least not since her mother died, and not before the marshal.

And not again. She swore to it.

JARED WATCHED the door close, and he wished he had something to throw. Some way to vent his frustration and anger and guilt.

He groaned. Damn, but he hurt in more than a few places. He'd strained his leg, and the wound throbbed like the blazes, but so did his groin.

Even more painful was the ache in his heart.

He'd listened to her try to explain what had just happened, but her eyes had said so much more. He wanted to take her in his arms—arm—and soothe those fears and uncertainties. He wanted to kiss her again. Dammit, he wanted his heart to come alive again. He'd believed it was better not to care, because then you didn't get hurt.

Now he realized the cost of the path he'd followed.

He hadn't really been alive. He'd gone through the motions, replacing his heart with duty. Replacing love with revenge.

Sarah would have hated that.

He looked down at the stains on the sheet. Her blood. His stains. It had taken every ounce of control in his body to pull out before he spilled his seed. He couldn't leave her with child. Not until he solved the question tearing him apart. Could he forget about MacDonald? Could he forget the man had killed Emma, had killed others in cold blood?

Jared knew he couldn't keep his badge if he did. It would violate every tenet of his oath. To the law, to himself.

He wondered whether she would return with fresh sheets. The image of her face when she left was burned into his mind. More wistful than sad. More puzzled than angry. More bewildered than tearful. Dignity intact. Dignity and pride and independence.

Damn, he loved that independence.

He admired that sense of loyalty, even if misplaced.

Heaven help him, but he feared he was falling in love with her. How could love happen in such a short time?

It hadn't. It was lust, he told himself. Just lust.

So why did his heart continue to ache?

MORNING CAME much too soon or maybe she just didn't want to face the day. And the marshal.

The sheets. She scurried out of bed, dressed hurriedly and grabbed several clean ones from another bedroom and ran down the steps. The coffeepot was cold, which meant Archie hadn't come down yet.

She grabbed the key to the marshal's room and went inside.

He was sleeping, the top sheet tossed on one side. She wanted to remain angry. She also wanted to touch him. To remember all those feelings from last night.

She put a hand on his shoulder, and he sprang awake, one hand going to his side as if reaching for a gun, the other pulled tight against the chain. He blinked, then focused on her.

"I...came to change the bed."

She felt embarrassed, by both her reason for being here and her own wanton behavior last night.

He raised a lazy eyebrow, then nodded. She had him roll over several times until she was done, then gathered up the soiled sheets.

"I'll bring you coffee later," she said.

"I'll be waiting," he replied seriously.

She didn't know whether he was laughing at her or being kind, or just trying to ignore last night. *She* decided to do the latter, though her heart beat so loudly he must have heard it.

Just as she was dumping the sheets with other washing to be done, she heard noises outside. A loud greeting.

She looked out.

Reese. Reese was back. Another gun. Another pair of eyes that might see what she didn't want anyone to see.

And another one of her godfathers.

She ran out the door, into the street, where she could really look at him. Slender as always. Tall. He was a handsome man with auburn hair and a fair complexion. Unlike Mac, he didn't seem to age, although gray edged his hairline under the expensive black hat.

He'd been gone two months, and he couldn't have arrived at a better time. Or a worse one.

"Sam, lass, but you're a sight for these weary eyes." He swung her up in his arms as he had when she was a kid. Not as high, but every bit as fast.

"You came through the pass this morning?" she asked when he set her down. She noticed now that he looked tired, older, and his usually immaculate clothes were wet and rumpled.

"Aye. I arrived at the pass last night, but the rain was still too heavy to chance it. I stayed in that old shack on the other side. Rode through at first light although it was hard going. Probably wouldn't have made it without my sure-footed Sally. She knows the trail better than I do."

He paused. "I saw Jake. He damned near shot me. He told me about Mac and that marshal. How's Mac?"

"Better, but Archie said he still can't ride. Maybe a few more days."

"I'd already heard some bastard was raising an army to get Mac. It's one reason I rode back, although I was on one hell of a winning streak. There was a lot of conversation in Central City. Someone saying there was big money to be made for capturing Mac. One guy was asking a lot of questions about this area, places to hide, and sure as Lucifer, someone told him about this place. Just like someone must have told that marshal." He looked at her. "Did you really shoot him like Jake said?"

She nodded.

"Where is he?"

She nodded toward the room. She tried not to show any emotion.

"I should have been here. You weren't hurt?"

"No. I might have been. He noticed I was a woman and hesitated."

Reese studied her closer. "I'll talk to him as soon as I get some dry clothes on." He paused, then said, "Can you heat some water? I could use a bath. I've been riding nonstop. I wanted to make sure you got out of here if you weren't already gone. Mac's wounds complicate things some."

"We just need a few days more."

"I don't think you can depend on that," he said.

"I've prepared the mine shaft. We can stay there several days."

"The marshal, too?"

How much had Jake told him? "I don't know."

"How badly injured is he?"

"His leg. I don't know if he can walk, but he's getting stronger. Archie handcuffed him to the bed. He's in the room they used to use as a cell. Mac doesn't know about him yet," she added. "We—Archie and I—were afraid he might try to go down…"

"Mac isn't going to like that," he said. "I wouldn't, either."

"You don't know how…sick he was."

"He's better now?"

"Some. But…"

"Tell me about the marshal."

She didn't want to talk about Jared… "Not much to tell. He's a marshal. He's been after Mac for a long time." She hesitated. Whatever she said would be a betrayal to either Mac or Jared. But Reese had to know. "He believes Mac killed his sister-in-law. He won't give up."

"Then we have to change his mind. Or," he added, "solve the problem for him."

Her heart stopped for a moment. She wasn't sure what he meant.

"Don't look so stricken, Sam," he said. "I don't want a marshal's blood on my hands."

"Then…how?"

"Let me think about it."

He wouldn't say anything else now, and she wanted to divert his attention from Jared. "How much did you win?"

"A little less than ten thousand dollars. Enough with your

gold to buy a good piece of land for ranching." His aristocratic features creased in a smile. "My luck came back."

"I hope it continues," she said.

"I'm going to get out of these wet clothes," he said, "then check on Mac. I want to meet this marshal, too. And I really don't like the idea of you being trapped in the mine. I heard they were looking to hire Jed Cantrell. He's the best tracker in Colorado. I think we should start thinking about the raft. It's still in place?"

"Yes, but the creek's not passable. Been getting higher with all this rain."

"We may not have a choice. I'm hearing that rancher raised fifteen, maybe twenty men. Believe me, they won't care who they shoot. There's a five-thousand-dollar bounty on his head." He flashed the devil-may-care grin he usually wore. "If Mac weren't my friend, I'd be mighty tempted myself."

She swallowed hard. She'd been worried, but nothing like she was now. "Got something to eat around here?" he asked, his gaze never leaving hers.

"Bacon. Some hard biscuits. Jam. Honey. I took most of the supplies to the mine."

"I'll go see Mac while the water's heating," he said, "and any food you have would be gratefully received."

She nodded, anxious for him to leave. Each time they mentioned the marshal, she was afraid the blood would rush to her face.

She filled a large pot and put it on to boil. Archie had already stuffed wood in the stove for the coffee and the embers were still burning. It would take a while to heat. In the meantime, she fried bacon and potatoes and heated yesterday's biscuits. Fear kept her moving. She'd halfway thought the marshal had been lying. She'd gone through the motions of preparing the mine shaft, but the need hadn't been entirely real. Now it was. Reese was concerned, and Reese didn't get concerned often.

Fear snaked up her spine, just as it had when she'd shot Jared. Fear not only for herself but for her three godfathers.

And Jared? What would Archie and Reese do about him?

She poured some coffee and fetched the key to the marshal's room. She wasn't surprised to see him awake. Did he ever sleep?

Light filtered in from the other room. She left the door open while she handed him the coffee, then lit the lantern on the table. It took all the willpower she had to look him directly in the eyes.

"You wanted to know who else lived here," she said. "My third godfather just arrived. He says your rancher has raised fifteen or twenty men along with a tracker."

He sat straighter. "You have to get out of here."

"I can't."

"Because of MacDonald?"

Her face must have supplied the answer.

"Would he let you die for him?"

"No." The familiar voice came from the doorway, and she whirled around to see Reese.

He had changed to a dry pair of clean dark pants and a white shirt, his usual deceptive smile in place. That and his British accent often fooled people into not taking him seriously. He could shoot every bit as well as Mac if necessary, though he preferred using his wits over violence.

"Evans?" he acknowledged.

Jared nodded. He shifted on the bed to a sitting position, gingerly lowering his wounded leg to the floor. "And who might you be?"

Reese turned to her. "I think that bacon might be burning," he said.

Sam didn't like the dismissal. She didn't want to leave. She wanted to hear what was being said.

Yet she did smell the bacon sizzling and they didn't have that much left to waste. Besides, any objection might raise more questions later. She wasn't ready for those.

When she'd warmed the biscuits, she opened a precious can of peach preserves and spooned out a third for Reese. There would be plenty left for Mac and Archie.

And the marshal.

She wished she was a fly on the wall inside that room. She wished the door wasn't so stout. She wished a million things, but she feared now that none of those wishes would come true.

She went over in her mind what Reese had said. Fifteen or twenty men. There were, at best, seven of them, including Jake and Ike. This wasn't their battle.

And the tracker could easily find the mine shaft. And the raft? Being buffeted on the swift-moving creek would be even more dangerous for Mac.

Would he let you die for him?

The marshal's question echoed in her head.

As did Reese's blunt reply.

Her hands shook as she turned over the bacon. Why had she allowed herself to be caught in some fantasy when the world was closing in on her and the men who made up her family?

15

JARED STARED at the man who'd just entered the room. He'd been surprised that Samantha had so meekly agreed to leave. He hadn't suspected meekness was in her.

"I'm Reese," his new visitor said. "I'm Mac's friend, and you might call me one of Sam's godfathers. That's what she always calls us."

"Are there any more?" Jared asked wryly.

"You've met Archie. You know about Mac. I'm the third and last."

Jared stared at him. He had an aristocratic bearing and his clean white shirt was well tailored. A bit fancy for his taste. As were the black trousers. The man's hair was beginning to gray, and Jake judged him to be in his forties. He had a slight English accent, but it was obvious he'd been in the country a long time.

"You need some clothes," Reese said, his gaze going to Jared's open shirt.

"It's hot as hell in here."

"And Sam has been in and out." It wasn't a question. More an observation.

Jared shrugged. "She's been looking after the leg."

"She said you think Mac killed a relative of yours."

"That's right. A very gentle young woman named Emma."

His visitor looked puzzled. "That doesn't sound like Mac.

He's a Southerner who respects women. His sister was raped, and it's always haunted him. I can't imagine him purposely hurting a woman, much less killing one. He never patronized my girls at the saloon, but treated them all like ladies. They adored him."

Damn, did everyone think MacDonald was some kind of saint? "There were witnesses," Jared said.

"When was this robbery?"

The day was burned into Jared's memory. "The fourteenth of January, 1866."

"You are wrong, then, Evans."

"I don't think so."

"I know so. I was with him then, and neither of us was killing anyone."

He said it with such utter confidence that it made Jared doubt himself for the first time. "How do you remember one day a decade ago?"

"Ask Sam when her mother died."

"Why?"

"Because it's one date I'll always remember. We were all there. Archie. Mac and myself. It was unusual. We weren't friends, but we knew each other. Mac rode in and out. Archie brought supplies back and forth and I had a part ownership in the saloon. We all helped Mary build a boardinghouse. She already fed half the town with an outdoor restaurant. She was a good investment as well as a very pretty woman."

Jared was silent. He knew liars. He didn't doubt that Reese had been one at times, but the emotion in his voice told him he wasn't lying now.

Reese stared at him thoughtfully, then continued. "We had an early snowstorm. Mary was caught in it. She was taking a meal to a sick miner who lived down on the creek. Apparently she got lost on the way back. The snow was blinding, and she'd walked off the trail.

"When we found her she was nearly dead. She caught pneumonia and died five days later on January twelfth, two days before your sister-in-law was killed. Mac was there when she asked us to take care of Sam. There was no one else, she said. She didn't want her daughter to go to a work farm or to strangers.

"We all agreed. Mac was the closest to Mary, although I tried like Lucifer to replace him. We both courted her, along with every single man in Gideon's Hope, but she loved Mac. After she died, he pretty much stayed put here and looked after Sam."

Nothing could have surprised Jared more. He mulled over what Reese had told him, then asked, "Why should I believe you about the date?"

"Mary was buried in the graveyard not far from here. Gideon's Hope was a thriving town then, and we had a stonemason. He made the marker. Flowers are growing there. Not newly planted flowers. The date of her death is carved on the stone. I think you will find those numbers have been there for a while."

"That doesn't prove MacDonald...Thornton...was here," Jared said.

"As I said, Gideon's Hope wasn't a ghost town then. There will be any number of people who attended her funeral two days later. Some of those who left went to Central City. Others to Denver. I'm sure I could find more than a few willing to swear that Mac was here."

"One of the outlaws swore Thornton killed a woman during the stagecoach robbery. A witness said he mentioned his name."

"You will have to ask the robber about that. I do know that some of the men who rode with him were not happy he left them. It might have been their revenge." He glanced down at the book on the bed. *"Les Misérables,"* he said. "Learn anything from that?"

"You've read it?"

"Oh, yes. I found it very...intriguing. A rigid, joyless man, the policeman."

Jared knew he was being baited, and it didn't help that he'd felt a twinge or two while reading the book. He hadn't reached the ending yet but he suspected from Reese's words that he wouldn't like the implied comparison.

He changed the subject. "Why stay here after everyone left?"

Reese shrugged. "These mountains were home to Archie. They were convenient to me. And as the miners left, Mac felt safe here. He knew there were posters out on him. I knew he had a past. I didn't ask about it, and he didn't tell me, but I know he was here on that particular day. As for moving, hell, I'd put everything I had into the saloon. Couldn't very well take it with us and there weren't many buyers. Mac had lost everything in the war. Archie never had much. The compromise was to stay in Gideon's Hope where we could all look after Sam until we could save enough money to start a ranch."

"But what about Sam? No children to play with. No school."

"And your interest is what?" Reese asked sharply. "Why should you care? I understand she shot you."

Jared shrugged. "She could have killed me. She didn't. She helped Smith do what they could to save my leg."

"You could arrest her."

"I could, but I won't."

"Why?"

"I admire loyalty."

"Nothing more?"

"What more could there be?"

"Come, Evans. You're not a dolt. Don't make the mistake of thinking I am. Man. Woman. She's been alone here with three old men for a long time."

Old or not, Reese was a fine-looking man. At least Jared thought women would think so. He would have called him a dandy if there hadn't been a deadly glint in his eyes. Again, he was confounded by the relationships. Was it really as simple as this man said? And if so, how would they view what happened last night?

"You might have noticed, I can't do much of anything,"

he said. "Smith made sure of that." He decided to stop being defensive. "Reese what?" he asked.

"Reese Hamilton at your service," he said with mock humility.

Jared had more questions. "You didn't say why you kept her here even after you 'buried' Thornton."

"Kept her? You don't keep Sam from doing anything. We wanted to send her to school. She wouldn't go. Threatened to run away and come back. And she would have. Both Mac and I have good educations. We both taught her. Our goal, particularly as Sam grew older, was to buy land in Montana. I've been there, and the grasslands are perfect for cattle. We decided that I would raise what I could gaming, Mac and Sam would pan for any gold that was left. Snow and flash floods constantly wash dust down the stream. Not enough to sustain a town, but over time we accumulated a good bit."

"Why didn't you leave then?"

"It was never enough, mainly. But I think it was really because none of us wanted to leave."

Jared studied him. He still had no idea why this man was answering all his questions. There had to be a reason. A really damned good reason.

"I saw how Sam looked when she talked about you," Reese said, as if he'd read Jared's mind. "I know how guilty she feels. She'd never shot so much as a rabbit before. That should tell you something about how she feels about Mac. I also know your reputation. You're a hard man, they say, but honest. And," he added slowly, "we may need your help."

Nothing could have startled Jared more.

Reese stared at him for a long time, then said softly, "There's fifteen or twenty top gun hands headed this way. They have a bloody good tracker with them. They were slowed while waiting out the storm, but they will be here soon. And Sam won't give Mac up. She'll die for him."

Jared swore to himself. He hadn't expected that many, and he'd still hoped to convince her to leave.

"I'd heard a rancher was raising gun hands. Your MacDonald

killed his son. I tried to warn Samantha, but she thought I was trying to scare her."

"I was in Central City when I heard. I've been riding day and night since. We have a day, maybe two. Not much more."

"Can you make her leave?"

"She can't. She won't." Reese hesitated, then added, "Mac is upstairs. He's too injured to leave now, and even if he could we would most likely run into them."

Upstairs. Damn. So the noise he'd heard several days ago *was* MacDonald. Not Archie.

"You could all be arrested for aiding a wanted outlaw."

"Aye, and Sam for shooting you." It was a dare.

Jared wondered whether the newcomer had heard or seen something in him to say those words.

"What do you want?" Jared asked.

"Basically we're trapped," Reese said. "We can't move Mac yet. The pass is one of two ways out. The other is down the creek—more of a river now—but that would be dangerous, too. The canyon walls are high and the water swift with the runoff from these storms. When those…bounty hunters arrive, they won't care who they kill. Or rape. I thought that might matter to you."

It did. Too much. Jared tried to absorb everything Reese had said, but what struck him deeper and more painfully was his last comment about Sam. And it was true.

Reese was a gambler, yet what he said had the ring of truth. "You could force her to leave."

"I could, but she would never forgive me, or worse, she'd never forgive herself for letting me do it."

"What do you want me to do?"

"I don't know yet. I wanted to take your measure first."

"I've been hunting MacDonald a long time," Jared said slowly, "and not only for the murder. There's a long list of robberies. But no one will take a prisoner from me."

"With a five-thousand-dollar reward on his head? They will kill you, then all of us, and claim Mac did it."

Probably true. "Who all is here?" Jared said.

"Mac. His gun hand is smashed and he's still feverish from other wounds. Archie, who can't see across the room. Burley, who couldn't aim straight if he wanted to. Sam. Then there's Jake and Ike. They're both old mountain men and loyal to the bone. Good shots. They're watching the pass now."

"That's it?"

"That's it," Reese replied.

"Have you talked to the others?"

"No. I wanted to speak with you first."

"And...?"

"I'm withholding judgment." He walked to the door, then turned. "Can't decide yet whether you're a blessing or a curse."

SAM HAD WAITED impatiently just outside the door. She jumped when it opened and Reese came out, closing and locking it behind him. He strode to the stove and lifted off the big pot of water.

"What happened?" she asked anxiously. Fear had settled deep inside her.

"You care about him, don't you?" he said, answering her question with one of his own.

"Yes."

"How much?"

"I don't know."

He gave her his cocky gambler's grin and kissed the top of her head. "I suspect you do know, but first I'm going to take that bath and eat something, then we'll have a council of war. Jake will let us know if anyone is coming."

She didn't want to wait, but she knew a bath wouldn't take him long, and she figured he needed time to think. He looked tired.

"The bacon's ready," she said. She quickly filled the biscuits with jam and loaded a plate with bacon and biscuits and canned fruit. "I'll take it up to your room."

She followed him upstairs to the largest and fanciest room

in the saloon. He poured the water into the hip bath, then took the plate from her, picking up a slice of bacon.

"You've been with him several times," he said, as if their conversation had never ended. "Do you think he can be trusted?"

"In what way?"

"All ways."

"I...want to think so. He's just so determined to take Mac in."

"Maybe not so much now." He told her about his conversation with Jared. "Mac couldn't have killed that woman. That was the year—the week—your mother died."

She remembered that week. How horrible it was. She'd been eleven, and her world collapsed.

"Did you tell him that?"

"I did."

"And?"

"I'm not sure he believed me, but he's thinking about it."

"What are *you* thinking?"

"A lot of things, but I have to talk to Mac and Archie. Now get out of here and take Mac some breakfast. He'll need it."

She wanted to demand answers but she knew Reese better than to ask. He wouldn't reply to her questions until he'd solved every problem in his mind, but for the first time she had hope.

Maybe the marshal, maybe Reese would tell her what they'd talked about.

She hurriedly put together a plate for Mac and placed it, along with two coffee cups, on a tray, then went up to Mac's room. She wasn't surprised to see Archie there.

Dawg greeted her and whined, complaining at being confined with Mac. She leaned down and scratched his ears. "I'll take you out. Promise."

Mac was awake and sitting up. His color was better, but there was still fresh blood on his bandages.

"What's eating at Reese?" he asked, his blue eyes darkening. "He was in here and said damned little. Something's going on. Has been for days, and I damn well want to know what it is."

She wanted to tell him everything. There was no sense in hiding it any longer.

But she would have to leave out one part.

16

FEAR, IMPATIENCE and frustration grew in Jared after Reese Hamilton's visit. It wasn't fear for himself but for Samantha.

Hamilton's words echoed in his head. She wouldn't leave MacDonald. And from what Hamilton said, their only defense against paid killers was a few wounded or aged protectors.

He wasn't much better. He wouldn't be able to move fast with his leg.

Damn those handcuffs. He twisted around so he could stand. Test the leg. He put two feet on the floor, then used the bedpost for support. Shards of pain shot through him, but the leg didn't give way.

The door opened and he turned toward it.

Samantha stood there. Her hair was mussed and she looked tired and worried. Something inside melted at the way her eyes lit when he looked at her.

She had to get out of the valley, even if he had to tie her up and carry her.

He held out his free arm, and she came to him. She rested her head against his shoulder as if she belonged there. Next to him. His arm tightened around her, and he held her closer. There was no regret, no hesitation. He struggled with an uncertainty that was new to him. Her trust against his lack of trust. Her belief in Mac, in him, when he no longer knew the meaning of the word.

Or maybe he was learning. He damn well wasn't going to lose her now.

"What did Reese say?" she asked after a moment of holding tight.

"That Benson's gunfighters aren't far behind him."

"And?"

"That I was wrong about your MacDonald."

She glanced up at him with hopeful eyes. "Do you believe him?"

"Let's say I'm considering it," he said. It was a lie. He did believe Reese Hamilton. The gambler wouldn't have lied about her mother's death or the grave. It could be too easily disproved.

He felt her release a breath.

"There's still other charges," he warned.

"But not murder," she said quickly.

"He's been accused of numerous robberies in the past ten years." He'd been thinking about this since Hamilton left. "But there's no real proof other than loose descriptions and hearsay. Except for the theft of military payrolls. He didn't bother trying to hide his identity."

She started to ask about that one, but a voice came from the doorway. "Now ain't this cozy?"

She spun around, but he didn't drop his arm. Archie Smith stood in the doorway. Reese was behind him. A third man, leaning heavily on Reese, was at his side. Jared recognized him from the posters, though his face was older. Dawg stood protectively next to the wounded man.

Jared lowered his arm then, but Samantha didn't move away.

Smith's face was red with anger. Reese Hamilton's expression hadn't changed since earlier, and Jared's quarry, Thornton/MacDonald, swayed unsteadily, supported by Reese. Jared was only too aware that the outlaw's gaze was taking in everything.

"Doesn't appear too injured," Reese commented.

"I think we should kill him now," Smith interjected.

"No," MacDonald said. "Reese, help me to the chair, then you and Archie pack up and get ready to leave."

His voice was surprisingly strong, although his arm was cradled in a sling and he seemed barely able to stand. Without comment, Reese helped him over to the one chair, and he sat.

"I would ask Sam to leave, but I don't think she's going to do it," the outlaw said.

Sam didn't move away from Jared. "No."

"Go, Archie," MacDonald said. "You and Reese gather all the ammunition we have."

Archie reluctantly left, and Reese gave MacDonald a searching look, then followed.

"Sit down," MacDonald ordered.

Jared obeyed. He didn't have a choice.

"You can sit at the end of the bed," MacDonald said pointedly to Samantha. Dawg looked from MacDonald to Sam, then padded over to her.

"You came for me," MacDonald said, his gaze meeting Jared's. "Reese told me about it. Not all, I suspect, but enough that I know what I want to do."

His voice was level, although Jared sensed the effort it took him to speak.

"First of all, I've...never killed a woman," Mac said. "I've committed some robberies, most of them army payrolls, and I'm ready to go back with you. I've been hiding long enough. I won't put Sam in danger ever again for something I did."

"There's the kid you killed a week or so ago," Jared pointed out.

"Kid, hell. Grown men. And they ambushed me. Three of them. I was protecting myself and the gold that Archie and Sam have been panning for nigh onto six years."

Jared had figured that quick enough. The men had not been deputized. They obviously wanted the reward, and the gold. He couldn't quarrel with a man protecting himself. He was beginning to understand why everyone was so protective of Mac. The man could barely sit up, and yet he was making the decisions and ready to go to a rope if it would save Sam. He was a far cry from what Jared had expected.

"We'll leave now," Mac said as he turned and glanced at Sam. "The marshal and I. Alone." He looked at her. "And no, Sam, you won't come. You will wait in the mine you were talking about. Archie will stay with you. Reese will shadow us, and when he feels we're clear, he'll come back for you."

"No," Sam said. "You can't ride yet."

"I can… I will."

"Even if it kills you?"

MacDonald looked straight into her eyes. "It *will* kill me if anything happens to you." He then looked at Jared. "Agreed?"

"*I'm* not agreed," Sam said. "If they have a tracker, they can find the mine shaft, and I expect they'll be very angry that you're not there. If you think I'll be safer there, you better think again."

"There's another option," MacDonald said. "Give myself up to them."

"No!" Sam's answer was as sharp as the sound of a shot.

Jared was still reluctant to change his mind about the man he'd hunted for so long. And yet it was obvious MacDonald considered Samantha more important than himself. He hadn't expected that. Maybe he'd been a marshal too long. Maybe he *was* becoming like the obsessed policeman in *Les Misérables*. Maybe he had become obsessed with vengeance and the letter of the law rather than compassion.

He weighed his options, and none of them were good. They could split their very small forces, him with MacDonald, and Sam with Archie. But she was right. A posse often was spurred by bloodlust. Deprived of their expected reward, they could well turn their anger on a woman and an old man.

He could take MacDonald up on his offer to give himself up to the posse. But he couldn't do that, either. Not only because Sam would never forgive him, but he could never forgive himself. He'd never lost a prisoner. He didn't intend to do that now.

"If you insist on taking Mac," Sam announced, "I'm going with you. I can use a gun."

"I've noticed," Jared said. But he knew she didn't trust him, that she feared he might push MacDonald too fast. He also realized the only way he could keep her here was to tie her hand and foot. That wasn't feasible, either.

She had that fierce look in her eye. Like a mama lion protecting her cub, but MacDonald was no cub. He sighed. "Trust me?" he said quietly.

He watched the struggle in her face. Despite what she'd said earlier, she didn't. Not entirely. Not when it came to MacDonald. He didn't expect the kick in the gut that came with that knowledge.

"He's not well enough to ride," she insisted without answering his plea.

"I've crisscrossed this state many times," he said. "I know trails no one else knows, and I'll make sure he gets plenty of rest. I can't be worrying about you, too."

He was aware of MacDonald glancing from his face to hers. The outlaw's expression was tense.

Archie entered without knocking. "We have all the ammunition together. And guns. Reese is saddling the horses. He and I talked. We all go together, make sure Mac gets a fair shake. I have a shotgun. If that fancy posse sees a group of five men, maybe seven with Jake and Ike, they might have second thoughts, especially if a marshal is with us. That shotgun's good to shoot a marshal, too, if needed," he added, glaring at Jared.

He fumbled in a pocket and brought out the key to the cuffs and unlocked them. "You betray Mac, and there will be three of us behind you until the day we kill you," he said.

Jared rubbed his wrist. "We should leave now," he said, not wanting more questions.

Archie nodded. "The horses should be ready. Sam, you grab the canteens and some hardtack and jerky. Best get your gun belt, too."

Jared had no more arguments. If Reese was right, they didn't have a minute to spare, and he had no doubt that Sam would follow them if they didn't let her come now. She would be in even more danger alone.

He nodded. Samantha hesitated.

He took her hand and squeezed it. "Trust me," he said.

She gave him a long, searching look, then dashed out.

SAM STARTED to gather food. Many of the supplies were in the mine shaft, but she grabbed the hardtack and jerky that remained and loaded them in flour bags. She filled canteens from the water pump and left them on the bar, then ran upstairs for an extra shirt and trousers to stuff into her saddlebags. After buckling on her gun belt, she grabbled her rifle and headed back down.

It hadn't taken more than a few minutes. When she reached the bottom of the stairs, she saw Mac leaning on Reese. Jared stood alone, but the lines in his face told her the effort it took.

Apprehension threatened to overwhelm her. Mac and Reese and Jared were not men easily rattled, but there was no mistaking the worry on their faces. A motley group at best. Only she and Reese weren't limping.

Jared wore the guns Archie had returned and Reese wore both a gun belt and carried a rifle. Archie carried a shotgun, and when they got outside she saw his whip on his saddle. Mac alone was unarmed.

She gave each of them a canteen and a cloth bag of hardtack and jerky. The horses and Archie's mule were all saddled.

Jared joined her. She knew from his face that he didn't want her to go with them.

"Could you stay if Mac was your father or brother?" she asked.

"No," he admitted, and she realized from his expression he was thinking of his wife and child.

She turned away, but he pulled her to him. His eyes ran over her, and she mentally cringed. She wore a shirt and pants with a hat pulled down over her forehead—the same clothes she'd had on when she shot him.

"You're beautiful," he said.

It was as if he knew exactly what she was thinking, but then she'd thought that before. His dark eyes told her he wanted to kiss her.

Ignoring the others, he put his fingers on her cheek. "Trust me," he said again as his gaze met hers.

And she did. At that moment she did. He had his gun. He had his freedom. He could have left them to the bounty hunters. She'd watched the change in his eyes as he and Mac had talked. And Reese, who was a fine judge of character, had given his trust, as well.

Jared was a marshal. He was bound by duty to take Mac in, but in this thing at least, she did trust him. He would get them out of Gideon's Hope. And then...

And then she would do what she had to do.

She moved away from him and toward her horse. She didn't wait for Jared to try to help her. God knew he could barely stand himself. She tied her saddlebags to the saddle, along with the sack of hardtack, then swung herself up as the others did the same.

They rode down the abandoned street, Dawg running alongside them. She heard a distant rifle shot, then a roaring noise from the direction of the pass.

Jake and Ike had unleashed the rock slide.

The bounty hunters had arrived.

17

"WHAT IN THE DEVIL was that?" Jared asked as he pulled up his horse and turned to Samantha.

"Rock slide," she said in a flat voice. "After you told me about bounty hunters, we rigged a pile of rocks above the pass. Once you start those going down, they pick up other rocks. Some friends, mountain men, have been watching the pass, ready to start a slide. Benson's men are here."

He remembered passing through on a trail barely large enough for a narrow wagon. He hadn't much liked the sight of boulders and rocks clinging to the cliffs. Not with the recent rain. "How were *you* planning to get out, then?" he asked.

"We thought a rock slide would give us some warning if they came," she replied. "We hoped the pass would be blocked long enough that they would just give up. If not, we could pick off some from the top of the pass, enough to scare them off."

"How long will it delay them?" he asked.

"Depends on how much rock was picked up on the way down," she said. "But Archie thinks it could be enough that they would need dynamite to get through."

He realized they—Archie and Sam—had thought it all out and had decided to take the risks for MacDonald. He was humbled by that kind of loyalty.

He looked around at what was left of the town. The saloon. The livery. A charred brick building on the other side of the street and a small wooden house. The porch sagged and the windows were broken.

But the buildings could be used as positions for a cross fire. He suspected the mountain men were good shots. Had to be if they'd survived this long. Life in the mountains was as hard as it could get.

"I want to go to the pass and see what the situation is," he said, his gaze moving from one man to the other and lingering on Sam's face. "Maybe I can reason with them. The rest of you stay here and take up positions in the saloon and stable. Maybe the pass wasn't blocked completely."

Reese hesitated. "That leg looks none too steady, and there will be some walking. Maybe I should go with you."

Jared wondered whether the gambler was worried he would abandon them. "No," he said. "If they break through, I want some protection for Sam and MacDonald." He didn't have to ask if Reese could shoot. He had the look of a man who could take care of himself.

"Then take Archie," Reese said. "He can show you the path up to the top."

"I can do that," Sam broke in.

"No," all three men said simultaneously.

Samantha frowned, and her eyes flashed rebellion. Jared wanted to reach out and touch her, but then he wouldn't be able to leave. And there was no time for those kind of feelings. Gideon's Hope could turn into a killing ground with Sam one of the casualties unless he found a way to control the situation.

He used the one weapon he knew would be effective. "Mac-Donald needs you here."

He watched the emotions play across her face. Then she nodded, and relief flooded him. He looked at MacDonald, at his heavily bandaged right hand. "Can you shoot with your left hand?" he asked.

"Not as good as the right, but I can get by."

Dammit, he had to trust the man. A galling thought after ten years of anger and pursuit. Still, Jared needed him. He turned, saw Sam's eyes on him and made the decision.

"You better use a rifle, MacDonald," he finally said. He realized then he was thinking of the outlaw now as MacDonald. Had been for the past several days. Not Thornton. Not a killer.

"Take the window on the first floor of the saloon," he continued. "Sam, you take the second-floor window on the far right. Reese, you take the loft in the stable. Establish a cross fire. Position any extra rifles so they're poking out the window. I want them to think we have more guns than we do."

He didn't want to give Samantha time to think, to argue. Hell, *he* didn't have any time to think. But Samantha was right about the mine. A tracker could easily locate them. There would be no way to cover the tracks with all the mud.

Jared turned toward the trail. Samantha guided her horse next to him. She turned her face up to his and her eyes had never been quite as bright. "Be careful," she whispered.

For the first time in years, he had every intention of being careful.

Archie led the way up to the path, and Jared followed. Once they left the main trail, they continued on a barely visible path up the mountain. The sound of rifle fire grew louder as they climbed the steep trail.

Then a whistle sang out.

"Jake," Archie explained. "He sees us."

At the top of the pass, Jared watched as a grizzled old man dressed in buckskins approached. He showed no friendliness as he studied Jared.

"That the marshal?" he asked Archie.

"Yep," Archie said. "How many?"

"Fifteen to my count. Kind of hard to say for sure since the rock slide scattered them. They're regrouping, though, and some are trying to clear the pass. Don't think they'll have much success. Saw one riding like hell toward the east. Wouldn't be surprised if he's after dynamite."

"That should give us another day or so," Jared said.

The mountain man directed his attention to Jared. His expression made it obvious he didn't hold marshals in high regard.

"We thought to stop 'em with a few shots, but they fired back, and some of 'em were damned good."

Jared dismounted awkwardly. Pain shot through his leg as he put weight on it. He limped to the edge of the cliff and looked down. A dozen men were trying to remove the rocks that blocked the pass. Several others were gathering horses that had been spooked. A bullet hit a rock next to him, and he ducked.

He looked at Archie's undershirt visible under his blue shirt. It was white. Or had been at one time. Now it was gray. "Give me a piece of that undershirt," he said, "and something to hang it on."

Archie started to protest, then shrugged as he understood. When he'd slipped out of it, he handed it to Jared, then quickly cut a branch with his knife. He watched silently as Jared tied the undershirt to the branch.

Jared waved the flag high enough that the men below could see it. "U.S. Marshal," he hollered down. "What do you want?"

"We want Cal Thornton," one shouted back.

"He's in my custody," Jared said. "He's been arrested and I'm taking him to trial."

"We'll do it for you," came the reply.

"I have a posse with me," Jared bluffed.

"Haven't heard of no posse. Just of a lone marshal traveling this way."

The men didn't slow their efforts to clear the rocks, and another bullet whizzed by Jared. He stepped back.

He had his answer. Still, he tried again. "Don't believe everything you hear," he yelled down.

He turned to the man called Jake. "You got more loose rocks?"

The man nodded. "Sure. Enough to jar some more boulders loose and mebbe hurt some of them. Not enough to block the pass again if they get dynamite."

Jared nodded. "Just give me what time you can."

Archie stepped closer to Jake. "You two skeedaddle if it looks like they're coming through. Warn us, then disappear up into those mountains."

"Hell you say," Jake said, and Ike nodded. "We owe Mac. When we roll out the next rock slide, we'll ride back down into town. Both of us are real good with rifles."

Mac the damn saint again.

Jake speared Jared with a glare as if he'd read his mind. "Make no mistake. You try to take Mac in after this is over, you gonna have trouble, and there's more of us than there is of you. And don't you go blame Sam none. She did what she had to do."

For a moment, Jared thought the man might take his rifle and shoot him right then.

Maybe he deserved it. Probably deserved it. He'd allowed his penis to override his good sense. He'd bedded a virgin, even knowing that he would take in the person she so obviously loved. There was no way she would forgive him for it, even if MacDonald agreed to go with him. The man faced serious charges even if he were cleared of murder. The army wasn't forgiving of payroll robberies. Prison was a certainty.

He thought of Sam back in that sorry excuse for a town she loved. She'd been ready to die for MacDonald. She still was ready. His heart thumped painfully in his chest.

He saw Archie watching him. Probing.

He took a step toward his horse, and his leg almost buckled. He had to be careful. The pain had receded as his mind concentrated on finding a solution, but his wound wasn't remotely healed and he was weaker than he'd thought.

"Need help?" Archie asked.

"No," he said. "Let's get down." He paused a moment. "You sure the creek is too dangerous?"

"Yep. We have a raft but it would be torn to pieces against the rocks."

Jared had to trust him on that. Archie had lived here for years and he wanted to get Sam and Mac out. If he said it was impossible, then it was. No one was going out that way, especially not an injured man.

He and Archie exchanged glances, then turned their horses toward the tiny cluster of buildings that was all that was left of Gideon's Hope.

Jared dismounted in front of the saloon and went inside. Mac-Donald tried to rise from a chair, but was none too steady.

"Stay down," Jared said. "Where's Sam?"

"Loading rifles and positioning them in rooms above," Mac-Donald said. "We have four extra rifles." He looked at Jared and raised an eyebrow in question. "How many men out there?"

"Fourteen...fifteen, maybe. A few looked like they were injured in the rock slide. One of your people up there says someone rode like hell toward Central City, and the others are digging. He thinks the rider probably went after dynamite."

"Unless they know what they're doing, they'll make things worse," MacDonald said. "If they do know how to handle explosives, they can get through pretty quick, but the nearest dynamite is about twenty-five miles away."

"We could try to pick them off," Archie said.

Jared had thought about that. But to shoot down they would have to reveal themselves, and the posse was composed of skilled gunmen. He also wasn't sure how much value Archie and MacDonald would be. That left the mountain men, himself and Reese. And Sam. She wouldn't be left behind. He knew that.

He didn't want wholesale slaughter. Nor did he think they had enough ammunition.

MacDonald stood. "That's it, then. I'm going to ride out to them. I'm not putting Sam and Archie in danger. They want me. No one else."

"You couldn't get through, either," Jared countered.

"No, but we could let them know I'll surrender when the pass is cleared."

"Hell you will," Jared said. "No one takes a prisoner from me. No one ever has, and no one will."

"What about Sam?" MacDonald replied tersely.

"You think she would ever have a good day again if you walked out of here to God knows what?" He hesitated, then added slowly, "I've lived with that kind of guilt for nigh onto ten years. It's not something I want Sam to carry."

MacDonald's eyes sharpened. "Better than her dying."

"I don't think she would agree," Jared said. "And maybe I can figure out a way to keep us all alive."

"I'm listening," MacDonald said tersely.

"What do you usually do when you have a rock slide?" Jared asked. "How do you clear it?"

"Dynamite. We have some left over from the mining days."

"Where is it?"

"In an old mine shaft. After the fire, we didn't want to keep it in town."

"How far?" Jared asked as new hope started to build inside.

"A few minutes by horseback. Archie can show you where it's located."

Jared said to Archie, "Let's go." He turned to Reese, who had joined them. "You stay here with MacDonald and Sam."

SAM WAS HALFWAY DOWN the stairs when she heard Mac's offer to give himself up to the hired guns and Jared's abrupt refusal to let him do so. She stopped to listen. Even as her heart cracked at his comment about the toll of guilt, she relished his next words. *It's not something I want Sam to carry.* He knew her. Understood her. Even more, he respected her and her loyalties. He may not agree with them, but...

She wanted to run down and hug him, but something prevented her. She didn't want him to know she'd eavesdropped. And she knew he still meant to take Mac in. She quietly went upstairs to one of the windows where she'd left a loaded rifle. She watched Jared ride away, Archie at his side on his mule.

Fifteen men, give or take. Experienced gunmen, if Jared and Reese were right. How could they hold off that many?

She went downstairs and joined Mac, who'd settled back into a chair. She suspected it was all he could do to keep upright.

She put a hand on his shoulder.

"I wish you weren't here," he said softly.

"I wouldn't be anywhere else."

"You like him, don't you?"

She suspected he already knew the answer. "Yes," she said.

"How much?"

"Too much," she said frankly.

"A marshal." Mac sounded disgusted.

"Not what I expected," she said with a grin.

"I don't want you...hurt."

"I won't be. We understand each other in a way. He knows I'll do anything to keep him from taking you, and I know that's what he feels he has to do."

"A conundrum," he said softly.

Conundrum. *A dilemma. A difficult problem.*

Except it was more than that. Much more. Her heart was involved.

Even now, she grew warm at the very thought of Jared. How could that be when...

Her hand tightened on Mac's shoulder. She owed him so much. And nothing good could come of today.

She was grateful he didn't ask more questions. She suspected he refrained because he already knew the answers. He wasn't one to rant or scold, just to be near if she needed something. She suddenly became aware of a wetness on her cheek.

She loved him so. She loved Reese and Archie, as well, but she'd never seen the guilt and pain in them that she saw in Mac. It weighed on him and had for years. She'd heard the same guilt in Jared's voice. The two men had far more in common than they would ever want to admit.

How long had it been? Fifteen minutes. Jared was probably at the mine now. The dynamite was old, unsteady. She moved closer to Mac. Closer to human contact.

They might die in the next few days. All of them.

JARED FOLLOWED Archie to the mine shaft.

"There's a bunch of abandoned mines along here," Archie

explained. "When the nuggets ran out, some believed there was gold in these mountains. Never found any veins, though. Me, I think it came down from far north."

It was probably the longest explanation he'd ever gotten from the old man. "How much farther?" he asked after several minutes of riding.

"We're here," Archie said, sliding off his mule.

The mine entrance was overgrown, but there was a path. Jared dismounted. It took him several seconds to get his balance, to adjust to the pain.

Archie appeared not to notice. "Some folks kept prospecting here after the town burned down. Didn't understand the gold came from up higher and was washed down." He took a hard look at Jared's face. "You be needing some help?"

Astonishing offer from a man who looked as if he could barely walk himself.

Jared shook his head, then followed Archie inside the mine shaft. The old man continued where he'd left off. "Them miners gave up before they went in very far," Archie said. He hesitated. "We thought about hiding Mac in one of the mines, and Sam stacked supplies there. But a good tracker could find it without much trouble. Durn mud."

More trust. More information. Jared knew Archie was right. There was no way to cover tracks, especially not in the time they had.

"What are you going to do about Mac?" Archie asked. "When we git him out of here."

Jared noted the man said *when,* not *if.* He wished he was as optimistic. "I don't know," he said honestly. Some ideas had been flirting in his mind, but his main goal now was to deal with the posse and get MacDonald and Samantha safely away.

Archie stopped at the back of the shaft and tossed aside a large piece of oilcloth. Jared quickly counted five boxes.

"Some of the dynamite is old," Archie warned. "Detonators are farther back. So are the fuse lines. There's two plungers."

"You know how to use them?"

"Some."

Jared thought it was probably more than "some," but he didn't push it. He stooped beside the boxes, and the strain on his leg almost caused him to fall. Pain shot through him. He muttered a curse, then asked Archie, "Got a knife? I seem to remember you took mine."

Archie handed him one. Jared opened the box and looked at the sticks of dynamite. "These boxes are too heavy for our mounts to carry."

"Not for my mule," Archie said. "She's used to heavy loads, and I know how to pack them. I'll walk alongside her."

Jared nodded. "I'll take the detonators and plungers with me."

Jared was surprised at how nimble Archie could be. He quickly but carefully packed the dynamite, two boxes on each side of the mule, and one on top. If there was any fear in the old man, Jared didn't see it.

As for himself, he had plenty of fear. He didn't like dynamite—especially aged dynamite—but placed strategically around town, it could make the difference between living and dying.

Once they arrived back at the stable, Archie carefully untied the ropes holding the boxes, and Jared helped him lower the dynamite to the ground. Archie handed Jared a shovel and grabbed another from the back of the stables.

Reese met them there. "All the guns and ammunition are distributed where you instructed."

Jared nodded and quickly explained what he wanted next. "We'll bury the dynamite in two locations near the hotel. Also in the back in case they try to surround the building. When the first riders approach, we'll set off the first round of dynamite in front of them. Let's hope the horses panic and unseat at least several of the riders."

He looked directly at Reese. "If they persist, we'll set off the second round. After that, we'll use the remaining sticks. I don't want them to get inside the saloon. Maybe by then they'll decide Benson isn't paying them enough."

"Jake and Ike can handle dynamite just fine," Archie broke in. "So can Burley. Used to be a fair miner."

"Okay," he said. He had come to trust Archie's judgment. "We have two plungers to activate the detonators," he said. "MacDonald will take care of the first one. Jake the second from across the street. Once MacDonald's plunger goes off, Burley should take it and rig the dynamite in back in case they decide to try to get in that way."

He didn't have to explain any more. Reese and Burley took a load of dynamite to the back, and Archie and Jared started burying the sticks of dynamite in the road running by the saloon.

Jared buried five before straightening up. Pain jabbed deeper in his leg, and he steadied himself on a shovel. He'd already abused his injury this day, and it was complaining like hell.

Then he noticed Sam several feet away, on her knees. Her hands were dirty and a speck of dirt sat on the end of her nose. She was so intent on the task that she apparently didn't notice him.

She shouldn't be messing with dynamite.

But he'd learned something these past few days. Sam would always be in the midst of life's battles. She would always be a rebel. It was who she was, and he...loved her for it.

He put a hand on her shoulder. She looked up at him with a lopsided grin. It was conspiratorial and confident. His fingers squeezed harder. How could he ever let her go, now that she had lodged herself in his heart? And how could he protect her, and still let her be Sam? How could he protect her—and MacDonald—without betraying a part of himself?

"Almost done?" Archie's querulous voice broke the silent bond between Sam and him.

Jared shot him a look that had quelled many a lawbreaker, but Archie wasn't fazed. The old man returned to digging holes, obviously expecting him to do the same. When they were finished, Jared attached the detonators under Archie's watchful eyes, and they ran the fuses into the saloon and attached them to the plunger. Then they started on the second set twenty feet south of the first.

He looked at the positioning of the dynamite again. Close. Really too close to the hotel. But Jared had only a few shooters and they needed to make every shot count. They couldn't afford to let the riders scatter. They needed them startled and contained in the middle of the street, close enough that every one of the defenders' bullets would count.

Now it would be a waiting game. He judged they had a day unless Benson's men were able to locate dynamite faster, and knew how to use it.

They should have a few hours' warning, but he wanted someone at the edge of town just in case something went wrong.

The rest of them could relax for a few hours. Rifles and handguns were loaded and placed where they should be. The dynamite was set. There was nothing else to do but wait.

"I'll scrounge something to eat," Sam said.

She never stopped. Most women would be needing comfort. Protection. Sam took care of herself and those she loved. She had fear. He'd seen it in her eyes. But she never let it slow her down.

Dammit, he loved her. Loved that quirky smile, and her sense of humor and the way she assaulted life. He loved the way *she* loved. Without condition. He loved the passion in her, and the loyalty. He hadn't understood it before, but seeing her with MacDonald, he now did. There was an unbreakable bond between the two of them. The man hadn't been pretending when he offered to go out there. He'd meant to do it. He still did. Jared saw it in his eyes.

They ate in silence. Bread and jam and cheese. Bacon. Beans. Three tins of canned peaches divided among the five of them. MacDonald ate lightly, and Jared could tell he was still in pain.

"You should get some rest," he said. "Archie, too. I'll take the first watch down the road, then Archie can take over in four hours. Then Reese. Fire two shots if you see anything that shouldn't be there."

"I can take my turn," MacDonald said.

"No," Jared said sharply. "You can barely move as it is, and we need you to get as much rest as you can for tomorrow."

Brief rebellion flashed in Mac's eyes, then disappeared, but Jared didn't think it had died. Still, the man needed help going up and down the steps. Jared took his own rifle and limped over to the livery to get his horse. He used a mounting block to ease himself into the saddle. Then he rode to the edge of town and stopped on a small rise where he could see the road that led to the pass. He dismounted and found a smooth boulder to sit on.

Not likely anyone could break through, and less likely that Jake or Ike wouldn't give adequate warning. But he needed to get away from the saloon, and Sam, and MacDonald. He needed to think.

The rain had stopped and the sky had opened. The first few stars of evening were glowing in a darkening sky. It was good to get out of that stifling room, to have his hand free. But now he longed to hold Sam with both arms. His conscience battled his heart. He'd found himself liking MacDonald. It was ironic after so many years of making the man the target of his anger.

Not exactly the man Jared thought he'd been hunting all these years. He knew he could clear Mac of the murder charges now. No question. But the others…

It was still his job to take him in.

And break Sam's heart.

He suddenly felt something cold and wet against his hand. He looked behind him and saw Dawg. Then Sam. Her smile was tentative, as if she was unsure whether she was welcome. He reached up and took her hand in his and pulled her down next to him.

They were quiet for a moment. He simply drank in her presence. There was always challenge in her, but there was peace, too. Her hand was small in his, belying her strength.

He released it and put his arm around her. Then both arms, and he held her tight. He couldn't endure it if anything happened to her, if that light inside her died.

"I wish you were out of this," he said.

"I—"

She was stopped by his lips. He knew what she was going to say. *I can take care of myself.*

There was an easy companionship between them. It had been there before in bits and pieces. The electricity was still there, too. Raw and vital and sizzling. "I can take care of myself," she said again, "but I need you." It was an admission he thought she would never make.

God help him, he needed her, too.

He pulled her to him, and her body arched against his. He pushed down her britches as she fumbled with his gun belt. Her shirt went next along with his pants and what was left of his long johns. She looked up at him and in the twilight her eyes were brilliant. Then they were on the damp grass.

The stars and moon glowed above them as they loved. Quietly and intensely. Even desperately. He didn't know what was going to happen in the next few days. And neither did she.

His hands moved over her, teasing, loving, caressing. Her body was soft and yielding against him, and he was only aware of the reality of her closeness, of the pleasure it gave him. Her body arched against his, and he was seized with elation and happiness. It faded quickly as he looked in her eyes, trusting and wondering, because their future was so uncertain.

But still he held her against him, not wanting to let her go. Touching. Feeling.

The fragility of their situation made every sensation more precious. Raw physical desire was still there, yet he had a fierce need to give rather than receive, and he savored the sound of her heartbeat, the taste of her, the gentle friction of skin against skin....

Sam relished the feel of his arms. Nothing else mattered at the moment. Her breath was gone, caught somewhere between her heart and throat as she looked into his eyes. They weren't cold or hard or distant now, but turbulent with want and need. Every nerve in her body seemed to purr, then he entered her slowly, deliberately, gliding in and out with rhythmic perfection. "Jared," she whispered, her voice hoarse with need.

His mouth covered hers as she caught his rhythm, and their bodies engaged in a primitive dance, her belly moving instinctively in circular motions, drawing him farther and farther inside. His strokes increased in power until she was riding a crest of a great wave, a giant force that swept her to the height of pleasure until she thought she could endure no more.

He gave one last drive that seemed to rock her entire being, and when she cried out in climax, he withdrew quickly and collapsed on top of her, his breath coming in rapid gasps.

He turned then on his side, holding her close as her body continued to quiver with aftershocks.

Jared put his arm around her. This was madness. Though they were on the farside of the hill from the ghost town, someone could come riding by. He had no doubt how Reese or Archie or MacDonald would feel about this. God knew they had enough problems without him complicating things.

He'd pulled out of her in time and he ached from that restraint. But he couldn't risk planting his seed in her until they had resolved things between them. Yet if he stayed like this... her head on his heart, her body radiating warmth...

He sat up, still holding her. Her body was damp from the moist ground, but the night was warm. He dressed her. Slowly. Gently.

"You should go," he said softly. "You need sleep."

"I want to stay with you."

"You'll be missed," he said. "I don't think now is the time for explanations." He softened the words with a kiss that moved from her nose to her lips.

"I...love you." She looked at him with that great earnestness that never failed to both touch and amuse him. She seemed surprised by her own declaration.

He closed his eyes. He had no illusions about what they faced. They were badly outnumbered. She was frightened for MacDonald. For all of them. When it was all over...

"Go," he whispered.

"You love me, too," she said.

He fought a smile. "Go."

And she did. Dawg looked at him for a moment, then, wagging his tail, he followed. But damn if Dawg hadn't looked like he was grinning.

SAM'S BODY HUMMED as she walked back to the saloon. She turned and looked at Jared, his silent form alert. Like a sentinel. And her heart wanted to burst with love.

Her body still quivered from the intensity of the sensations that had racked her body and the emotions that savaged her heart. She had given him everything she had tonight, including her trust.

Fear had heightened those sensations. Fear for all of them, but watching him now, she felt a new confidence. She remembered the efficiency with which he directed the planting of the dynamite. Everyone, even Reese, had followed directions without question.

And Mac...she had seen the changes in him as he talked to Mac. Jared was no longer the lawman or prosecutor. There had been a certain acceptance between the two men.

But could Jared give up being a marshal...?

18

SAM HAD JUST FINISHED preparing breakfast when they heard an explosion.

All of them rushed to the door, Mac being the last. Smoke was coming up from the pass.

Dynamite. The posse had gotten it faster than they'd hoped.

She met Jared's eyes. She'd been avoiding him this morning, afraid that her godfathers would see something different in her. In them. If they did, they didn't say anything.

Minutes later, Ike came tearing down the road on his horse. "We have mebbe thirty minutes," he said. "Someone knew how to use dynamite. Placed the charges just right. They're clearing a path now. Jake's started another rock slide but ain't nothing like the first."

"Come inside the saloon," Jared said. "Someone get Burley." He led the way and Reese fell in beside him. Archie veered off toward the stable. Minutes later Jared had everyone in the saloon, including MacDonald and Sam.

He wished like hell he could hide her away. His eyes met hers, and she shook her head. She knew exactly what he was thinking. When did that happen?

He forced himself to focus on the battle ahead.

"They expect a lone marshal and wounded outlaw," he said. "They don't expect an army, so we're going to give them an army. They want easy money. I want to make it very hard. I want guns propped up in every window we have. I want dynamite going off in different places. I want confusion. They have to believe they're outnumbered or, at least, that we have the defensive advantage."

He looked at Ike. "Ike, you take the stable across the street, and when Jake gets here, he should take the hayloft. You're also in charge of setting off the second round of dynamite. MacDonald is responsible for the first. Once the dynamite goes off, move from opening to opening. Make every shot count." He turned to Burley. "You watch the back. Once the first charges go off, you come get the plunger from MacDonald, take it to the back and rig the fuses. Archie will show you how."

Burley straightened. "Ain't no need for that. I was a miner." He looked at his hands. "They be steady now. I haven't had a drink in weeks."

Jared nodded. He had to trust Burley, just like he had to trust the rest of his ragtail gang of outlaws and misfits. He looked around. "We'll have to change positions. Reese, Sam and MacDonald at the saloon. MacDonald can use the rifle after he sets off the dynamite. Reese will move from window to window." He looked at Sam. "Sam, you just keep the weapons loaded. Don't get in the windows." It was the best he could think of to keep her safe. Or safer. But he saw the rebellion in her eyes. He ignored it for a moment. "If they get too close, throw the sticks of dynamite. That will make them damn wary."

"What about you?" Reese asked.

"I'll try to talk to them again when they ride in," he said. "I'll give them a chance to leave. If they see enough rifles poking out of windows…"

"No," Samantha said. "They'll gun you down."

"You gave them their chance," Ike protested.

MacDonald stood. He swayed slightly. "There isn't going to be a gunfight. I'm going to ride out to meet them. There's no sense in you all dying. Rope's waiting for me, anyway."

"No!" Sam said.

MacDonald's eyes gentled. "Ah, darlin' girl, I should have sent you away a long time ago. I was damned selfish."

"MacDonald's not going anywhere," Jared said harshly. "I don't give in to vigilantes or hired guns." He fixed his gaze on the man, then Samantha. "We're wasting time. Any more questions?"

No one said anything.

Reese went upstairs.

MacDonald had remained seated in a chair. He turned and looked out the window.

Jared limped over to Sam. He brought her chin up with his finger. "I wish you would go to one of the mine shafts."

"I can't."

"Then promise me to be careful. Keep your head down and load the guns. If things go bad, do you have a place to hide?"

She nodded, but he didn't believe her. She would be there to the end. Again he thought about grabbing her and cuffing her to the bed in the makeshift cell, but then she would be helpless if the gunfighters somehow got inside.

"Thank you," she said softly.

"For what?"

"Not giving up Mac. For trusting me."

His fingers ran up her face. "If anything happened to you…"

"Then it would be my decision," she said. "This is where I want to be. Where I have to be."

"I know." And he did. If anything happened to her, he didn't know whether he could live with himself. But if he didn't include her, he would destroy something inside her.

He leaned down and kissed her. He didn't care if Mac watched, or anyone else. Her arms went around his neck and she stood on tiptoes and kissed him back. Hard. Fervently. Then she let go and ran upstairs. Her scent remained with him, as did her touch.

MacDonald started to say something, but a rifle shot stopped him. *Reese was warning them.*

Jared stepped out and started down the street. His Colt was

in his holster, and he'd tucked one of Mac's spare pistols in his belt. He glanced around and counted at least ten rifles propped in the windows. They looked ready for action.

He took a few more steps, trying not to let the limp show. He wanted to get at least fifteen feet in front of the first dynamite sticks. It took all his concentration.

He stopped at the predetermined position. Not in the middle of the street but more to the side. An empty water trough was inches away. He stood and waited. This last attempt at peace was probably futile, but it was his duty to avoid bloodshed if he could.

The riders came in slowly, cautious. He saw them stop at the edge of town, their gazes searching the few buildings. One pointed to a rifle in a window, then another. They kept coming.

The leader appeared to be the heavy, bearded man. Jared knew the tracker who rode at his side. They stopped twelve feet from him and he watched as some of the posse placed hands on their gun butts.

"Thought you had better taste," he said to the tracker.

"It's a job," the tracker said. "Didn't think you would be protecting a killer."

"That's yet to be decided. I'm on the side of the law, and every marshal in the territory will hunt each of you down if you kill one of theirs. We don't forget and we don't give up."

"We don't want trouble," the big man said. "We just want my son's killer."

Benson. "No," Jared said flatly. "Look around. I have more than enough guns backing me." He watched as they took note of the rifles. Some of the men dropped their hands from their guns. "I don't know how much Benson offered you," Jared continued as he searched the faces of the men in front of him, "but I guarantee it's not enough for the trouble you face."

"I didn't sign up for killing no marshal," one man said. He backed up his horse and turned in the other direction. Three others followed him.

"Cowards," yelled Benson. "He's protecting my son's

murderer." He drew and fired as Jared leaped behind the trough. Adrenaline dulled the pain in his leg, but he knew he couldn't depend on it to support him. He felt a dampness and looked down. A bullet had nicked his right leg again.

Explosions ripped through the street just feet from the horses. At least a third of them reared, throwing off their riders and racing back toward the pass.

The remaining gunmen struggled to control their horses. Rifles fired from the saloon, stable and abandoned house. Several men fell.

Benson tried to rally his posse. "Five hundred dollars to every man who stays, and twenty thousand to the one who takes Thornton." Men about to ride away turned back.

"The marshal," the leader said. "Take the marshal. Surround him."

Jared knew he was in trouble. He had damned little protection. It had probably been a stupid thing to do, to walk out, but he'd had to try it. He knew the tracker. He'd hoped if he could convince him, he could turn the others.

He heard more explosions, but they were farther down the street. They startled the horses but only one man was unseated this time. Riders began to circle him. He drew and fired, and a man went down. Another man was felled before he could fire again. Reese? Archie?

"No!" A woman's voice sounded above the melee. He turned, as did the riders.

MacDonald stood in the middle of the street, cradling the rifle with his ruined right arm. His left fingers were on the trigger. He swayed slightly with the effort.

Jared knew instantly what he intended to do. Jared was trapped. MacDonald was giving him a chance at the cost of his own life. He was gambling that once he was dead, the vigilantes would quit.

Jared knew differently. He had seen the faces. They couldn't afford to let him live now.

Before he could react, Samantha ran out the saloon door, Colt in hand.

"No," MacDonald yelled like a man in pain. He dropped the rifle and threw her to the ground, covering her body with his, just as two shots rang out.

Jared turned and fired three bullets at the leader. The big man fell from his horse. More shots rang out from the saloon, the livery and the house. One man fell from his horse, then another. The rest dropped their guns and put their hands up.

Jared stood awkwardly, his gun in hand. "The first man that moves is dead."

Jared limped as quickly as he could over to MacDonald. Blood spread out from his back. Jared checked his pulse. Still alive. He felt him stir. "Don't move," he said in a low voice. "Play dead."

He lifted MacDonald gently from Samantha. She was bloodied from Mac's wound but her eyes flickered. The wind had been knocked out of her. Nothing more. Thank God. He pretended to be listening to her heart. "Play dead," he whispered. "For MacDonald." Her eyes flickered and he knew she understood. He picked her up. Her hat fell off and her shirt stretched tight over her breasts. He could hear the exclamations from the horsemen.

"Your friend just killed a woman, along with Thornton. You attacked a U.S. Marshal. I can't take you all in, but by God I've looked at every one of your faces, and you'd better make tracks out of this territory."

Slowly, one by one they turned to leave. With the leader gone, several of their posse on the ground and rifles still protruding out of windows, they had no more stomach for the business. Two dismounted and helped the wounded on horses, then they put their leader's body on his horse. They turned and galloped toward the pass as if the devil was after them.

Jared lowered Samantha to the ground and scanned her body as she protested, obviously wanting to get over to MacDonald. "Stay still," he warned.

Archie hobbled toward them, his bag in his hand.

Jared searched the road ahead. The riders were all gone.

Archie examined MacDonald, who bore it with the patience of a man too used to wounds.

"That man has more lives than a durn cat," Archie grumbled. "Bullet went through his side. Don't think it hit anything bad."

Reese appeared along with Jake and Ike. Reese and Ike, the two strongest, carried Mac inside. Sam shook herself as if surprised to be alive.

Jared took her in his arms. "You've got to stop doing this," he scolded, his voice breaking.

"You, too," she said, looking him over. "I think you're bleeding again." She hesitated, then added, "That was a damn fool thing for you to do."

He *was* bleeding, but at the moment nothing mattered more than feeling her in his arms. Knowing she was still alive. Unhurt.

"How's Mac?"

"You must mean Thornton," he said slowly. "He just died. So did you. There were at least ten witnesses, not including Reese and Ike and Jake and Burley. Maybe no one cares about Thornton, but they know they could hang for killing you. We shouldn't have any more trouble."

She searched his face, then closed her eyes. "Thank you."

"Seems to me you two saved my life, as well." He nuzzled her cheek. "But I have another problem."

"What?" she asked in a breathless voice.

"I think I'm in love with a sprite who doesn't know how to stay out of trouble." He wanted to caress every part of her. He tried to resist. Foolish thought. "I'm afraid I have to keep you with me to keep you safe."

"Look where that has gotten me so far," she replied, snuggling herself farther into his arms. "I think we might be dangerous for each other."

"I can live with it," he said. He eased away from her slightly. "Can you?"

She lifted her face to look up at him. Tumultuous emotions

shone in her eyes, and he lowered his head until their lips met in an explosion as bright as lightning striking the earth.

He didn't need a better answer.

Epilogue

"IT'S AS BEAUTIFUL as Colorado," Samantha said. She stood with Jared in front of their new home and watched the clouds float by in the biggest sky she'd ever seen.

Cattle munched rich grass along the river. Their cattle.

They'd found their ranch land three months earlier and filed claims for it under the Homestead Act. Today her home was finally finished and the last of the furniture moved in, including a cradle Archie made. The godfathers were celebrating with a picnic, but Sam and Jared had broken away for a quiet moment.

Sam felt Jared's hands on her shoulder as they gazed over the grasslands and the river that bordered it. Then those hands went around her swelling middle. She was four months along now. The three godfathers and Burley, who'd helped put in the last of the glass windows, were, to say the least, delighted.

They—the six of them—now had five homesteads, one hundred and sixty acres each, for a total of eight hundred acres. Beyond their homestead was open range, allowing them to own a large cattle herd. She and Jared had filed together since they were married on the trail when they met up with a circuit preacher. Archie, Burley, Reese and Mac had filed separate claims, all touching one another. She and Jared were given the best piece of land, the top of a hill overlooking the river.

To keep the claims, they had to build a house of some kind on their property. Burley had a one-room cabin. Mac had two rooms, but he planned on building more. Now that Thornton was good and truly dead, he had his eye on a pretty widowed dressmaker in the closest town.

Reese built a substantial one-room home, but he had plans to keep adding to it, as well. He'd limited his gaming to the saloon in the nearest town, but she felt sure his wanderlust would soon take him to the mining towns.

Archie built a little two-room building, half of which he used as a medical office. Sam usually helped him. There were no regular doctors within fifty miles, and both of them had been in high demand.

She and Jared had taken more time to build their place. He'd wanted a house that would stand for a hundred years, he said, and one big enough for a family. He was tired of wandering. Their home had one room large enough to entertain at least four frequent visitors and any additional family members, a large bedroom for her and Jared, a kitchen and two additional bedrooms, along with a loft.

"For guests," Jared said, "until family fills it." He made it clear he meant the godfathers. Their house was always open to them. The four men had worked well on their way to Montana; they'd become good friends as well as partners in the ranch.

She loved the land, but then she would love anyplace where Jared was. Jared and the godfathers. They had used their collective money to buy cattle. They bought some along the way, then several hundred more head from a rancher in south Montana.

Jared leaned down and kissed her neck. He couldn't seem to stop touching her, but that was all right. She couldn't stop touching him, either. She'd fallen in love with him quickly, but now she loved him deeply and thoroughly and unconditionally. She knew the difference now. Loving meant trusting. Loving meant believing. Loving meant forever.

He'd left after that violent day, and she and Mac had retreated to the mine shaft for several weeks. It was possible the law, or some of those men, would return. Jared thought it doubtful, though. Benson was dead, and one of the posse had taken the body home. He'd been killed by a U.S. Marshal. Dead along with a wanted outlaw named Thornton and a woman called Samantha Blair. They were buried in the same cemetery as her mother and father. Jared had made sure the news was in all the papers and he'd made the report to his superiors in Denver. Then he resigned.

Then he'd returned to Gideon's Hope for Sam and the others. They were his family, as well, now. An outlaw, a cardsharp and a cussing mule skinner. And Burley, who swore he wouldn't drink anymore—the devil had been plumb scared out of him. Jake and Ike stayed behind. Like Jake said, he wanted to be buried looking toward the mountains he loved.

She felt his fingers in her hair. She was letting it grow out. And she was wearing a dress. She found it more comfortable now that she was expecting. And she liked looking pretty for Jared. After the baby, though, she told him right enough that she was going to wear britches when she rode.

"They say there's hard winters," he said.

She grinned up at him. "Better, then, to stay inside and—"

He stopped the last word with a kiss. She barely heard the snickers behind her as once more her world spun to magical places and she melted against him.

She was home.

* * * * *

COMING NEXT MONTH

Available September 28, 2010

HARLEQUIN®

A *Romance*

FOR EVERY MOOD™

Spotlight on

Inspirational

Wholesome romances
that touch the heart and soul.

See the next page
to enjoy a sneak peek from
the Love Inspired® inspirational series.

*See below for a sneak peek at
our inspirational line, Love Inspired®.
Introducing HIS HOLIDAY BRIDE
by bestselling author Jillian Hart*

Autumn Granger gave her horse rein to slide toward the town's new sheriff.

"Hey, there." The man in a brand-new Stetson, black T-shirt, jeans and riding boots held up a hand in greeting. He stepped away from his four-wheel drive with "Sheriff" in black on the doors and waded through the grasses. "I'm new around here."

"I'm Autumn Granger."

"Nice to meet you, Miss Granger. I'm Ford Sherman, from Chicago." He knuckled back his hat, revealing the most handsome face she'd ever seen. Big blue eyes contrasted with his sun-tanned complexion.

"I'm guessing you haven't seen much open land. Out here, you've got to keep an eye on cows or they're going to tear your vehicle apart."

"What?" He whipped around. Sure enough, mammoth black-and-white creatures had started to gnaw on his four-wheel drive. They clustered like a mob, mouths and tongues and teeth bent on destruction. One cow tried to pry the wiper off the windshield, another chewed on the side mirror. Several leaned through the open window, licking the seats.

"Move along, little dogie." He didn't know the first thing about cattle.

The entire herd swiveled their heads to study him curiously. Not a single hoof shifted. The animals soon returned to chewing, licking, digging through his possessions.

Autumn laughed, a warm and wonderful sound. "Thanks,

I needed that." She then pulled a bag from behind her saddle and waved it at the cows. "Look what I have, guys. Cookies."

Cows swung in her direction, and dozens of liquid brown eyes brightened with cookie hopes. As she circled the car, the cattle bounded after her. The earth shook with the force of their powerful hooves.

"Next time, you're on your own, city boy." She tipped her hat. The cowgirl stayed on his mind, the sweetest thing he had ever seen.

*Will Ford be able to stick it out in the country
to find out more about Autumn?
Find out in HIS HOLIDAY BRIDE
by bestselling author Jillian Hart,
available in October 2010
only from Love Inspired®.*